Second Chance VOW

WALL STREET JOURNAL & USA TODAY BESTSELLING AUTHOR

M. ROBINSON

M. ROBINSON

SECOND CHANCE VOW

WALL STREET JOURNAL & USA TODAY BESTSELLING AUTHOR

M. ROBINSON

This book is a work of fiction. References to real people, events, establishments, organizations, or locations are intended only to provide a sense of authenticity and are used fictitiously. All characters are a figment of the author's imagination, and all incidents and dialogue are drawn from the author's mind's eye and are not to be interpreted as real. Though several people, places, and events portrayed in this book are correct, the story is fiction that the author has made up for entertainment purposes only.

DEDICATION

To Rachel Van Dyken

I will forever be grateful to have you in my life. I wrote this book fast and I swear it's because you trained me to. You write at the speed of lightning, and when we're writing together I need to keep your speed, so you're not waiting on me, lol! I love you so much, and I'm so thankful for our friendship, our random talks, our heartfelt ones, our laughs, and even our cries. Everyone needs a friend like you, you're one in a million.

I love you, bestie!

PROLOGUE

CHRISTIAN

Now

"I fucking love you, Kinley, and you know it."

"It's not about loving me, Christian. I love you with everything I am, but sometimes … it's just not enough. I can't live like this anymore. It's not fair to either of us."

"I don't give up on anything, Kins. Especially you."

She sighed, bowing her head.

I couldn't believe we were having this argument at my little sister's wedding. She was marrying my best friend, and this was supposed to be their day. I thought … fuck, I didn't know what I thought anymore.

How could we let life just get in the way of our love for each other?

We'd been together since we were fifteen. Married at twenty-four, and I knew she was the one I wanted to spend the rest of my life with. I wasn't going to risk losing her for anything, so I asked her to marry me and never looked back.

Ten years ago, we were so in love.

So devoted.

So fucking consumed with each other.

Where did we go wrong?

With the most sincere, pained expression on her face, she coaxed, "I don't want to be just another challenge or obstacle, something you don't give up on, Christian."

"You're taking my words out of context, Kinley."

"Am I? I haven't been your priority in who knows how long."

"That's bullshit! I'm inside you making you come on my cock—"

"This isn't about sex, Christian! This has nothing to do with that!"

"What the fuck? I give you everything! What more do you want from me?"

"You give me everything? You can't be serious. You think I don't realize how detached you are from me because I can't—"

"We are not talking about this here," I snarled in a low rumble. Gripping onto her arm, I dragged her ass to the back of the farmhouse on my sister's property where the ceremony and reception were being held.

During the exchange of their vows, we watched my sister and my best friend's new beginning while my world was crashing to a devastating end. And all I could do was sit there and stare at Kinley's face, desperately trying to hold onto the good times, memories of our life together.

I could see in her bright green eyes that I'd loved for as long as I could remember, her thoughts reflected my own—remembering a time when we were the ones standing in front of our friends and family, vowing to be together for better or for worse. She still loved me.

I still loved her.

Yet none of it mattered anymore.

Life had passed us by in the blink of an eye. We were no longer those two crazy kids who thought we could take the world on together. Our love had been replaced with anger, our devotion began to crumble, and our lives started drifting apart.

But anything worth having is worth fighting for, right?

She was the only woman who had ever touched my heart, my soul, and every fiber of my being belonged to her.

I was hers.

Inside and out.

However, now her love felt like a double-edged sword speared directly into my heart.

Her eyes weren't a bright, shiny shade of green. They looked sad and hollow, although I could still see the love she had for me hidden behind the depths of her uncertainty.

She turned around to leave, and I grabbed her arm, turning her to face me. "I love you, Kinley."

She immediately shut her eyes as if it pained her to look at me. I reached up instead, holding onto the sides of her face, willing her to open them for me.

"Sweetness," I tenderly coaxed.

I only called her that when I really needed her to look at me, to talk to me, to listen to me…

To feel me.

"I love you," I breathed out close to her lips. "I love you so fucking much, and you know that, baby. I saw your face during their vows. You can't hide from me. I know you were remembering our wedding day. How I looked at you when you were walking down the aisle. From the moment you walked into that church you took my breath away, and ten years later you're still taking it away. Don't you remember how I used to make you feel, Kins? Please, babe, tell me you remember how we used to be?"

She sucked in a breath as I wiped away her tears with my thumbs. "What happened to us? We used to be so fucking happy, so in love. You remember, don't you?"

—Kinley—

I cried, "Of course I remember." I'd never be able to forget. He was in my veins, in my blood, imprinted so deep in my bones I didn't know where I began and he ended. "You protected me. You're always protecting me, Christian, but you can't protect me from this—from what we've become."

"I loved you then. I love you now." He kissed the tip of my nose. "I'll love you always."

"You love what we used to be, not what we are now. It's over. You know it's over."

We had to be. I couldn't continue to allow him to sacrifice more than he already had for me. It wasn't fair what I was doing to him and had been putting him through every month for the last couple of years. I had to stop being selfish and put his needs and wants first.

I loved him enough to let him go, knowing I could never give him what he truly yearned for. I tried…

But I was broken.

He shook his head. "I don't want this for us, and I know you don't want it either. We're still here, sweetness. Deep inside, it's still us."

"Christian, please… I'm not trying to hurt you. It's the opposite—I'm trying to set you free. I'm just so fucking exhausted from disappointing you all the time. I can't live like this anymore."

"Well, I can't live without you."

I opened my eyes, revealing our life together in my devastated expression. It was the least I could do. This was killing me too. I didn't want this, but I didn't have another choice. I'd made the wrong one over ten years ago, and it had cost me the love of my life.

"How do I look at the woman I love and just walk away from her? Huh? Please tell me, Kins, because I have not a fucking clue."

I swallowed hard while more tears slid down my cheeks. "I know you blame me."

"That's not true."

"Yes, it is. I can see right through you. I always have, and I always will. I wish I could change things. If I could go back… Fuck, I just can't do this anymore. I've spent years regretting what I can't change, and now I see it in the way you look at me, in the way you talk to me. You blame me, Christian, so stop pretending like you don't."

"I don't care anymore. We'll work through it."

"All you'd be doing is settling for me, and I can't do that to you. We've been trying to make it work for years. Enough is enough. You have to let me go."

"The fuck I do."

I shoved him. "Stop! Just stop! We agreed!"

"What other choice did you give me?"

"The only choice we have left!"

"That's not the answer!"

Our chests were rising and falling in unison which was the only thing in sync with us.

"How can you not see it? What you're doing to yourself, to me—to us?"

I jerked back, his questions knocking the wind out of me. "What do you want me to do?"

"Fight for us!"

"I can't more than I already have, Christian! I have no fight left in me! It's all been taken away with every—" I stopped myself, unable to say the words.

It hurt too fucking much.

"Christian! I can't be here! I need to leave!"

"For fuck's sake, Kinley! You can't leave my little sister's wedding!"

"I don't care! It's your fault that no one knows the truth, and the longer I'm here, the harder it is to not tell everyone!"

Despite not wanting him to say the words, there was no holding back the fury soaring through his body as he spewed, "We're not ruining their wedding because you want to tell everyone right now that we're getting a divorce!"

"Yes! I do want to tell everyone! It's time! We've been hiding it for months! For years we've been pretending to be something we're not, and I can't do it anymore! For once can you just listen to me? Can you just see things through my eyes? You can't protect me anymore! I'm not that young girl you found in the woods! Why can't you see that?!"

"You'll always be that girl to me. You may have forgotten her, but she's never left my side. You've never left me, and you never will. Do you understand me?"

"Christian, we're not an us anymore."

"We'll always be an us, Kins. From the first time I claimed your lips, you were mine."

He did the only thing he could in a moment that felt as if we were saying goodbye. Gripping onto the back of my neck, he slammed his lips against my mouth, kissing me like he did that night all those years ago. He was desperately trying to remind me of who we used to be.

Except when we pulled away, resting our foreheads on each other for support, I wept, "I don't want to be yours anymore… It hurts too much."

I lied.

Not for me.

Not for us.

For him.

It was my turn to protect him…

From me.

My mind was thrown right back to that night when I found my soulmate at fifteen, in the woods, where he protected me, and he…

Made me believe in love at first sight.

Then

"You need to slow down on the whiskey, Kinley, or you're going to be sick," my best friend Jax warned, standing beside me out in the woods.

I was trying to enjoy the end of the year party. This was where everyone from several schools always gathered in our small town of Fort Worth, Texas.

"Jax, it's the last day of our freshman year of high school! We're officially Sophomores and made it yet another year at good ol' Adams High. Why can't you just live a little and enjoy it?"

"We both know you're not hammering down that bottle because it's the beginning of summer break, Kinley."

I rolled my eyes. "I'm not talking about this."

"I know. You never want to talk about your mom."

"That's because there's nothing to talk about."

"She wants to see you. That's not nothing."

"I have nothing to say to her."

"You haven't seen or spoken to her since you moved here with your aunt when we were in sixth grade."

I was originally from Ohio before my aunt moved us here, wanting us to start over. Her words, not mine. There was no starting over for me, not with what my mother had put me through since I was born. Back in Ohio, I had no one until my aunt got involved. Here, I only had her and Jax.

"You mean when she lost custody of me, and I had to go live with my aunt or just be another abandoned kid thrown into the system?"

He sighed deeply, knowing I was right.

Jax wasn't going to win this argument. My mother could try to reach me until she was blue in the face, but I wasn't going to give her the time of day. In my eyes, she was as good as dead like my sperm donor of a father was.

I'd never met him. He skipped out on us after she'd told him she was pregnant with me. At least that was what she always said when I'd ask her about him. Although, I didn't ask often. Especially as I got older and realized what my mother was.

"Listen," Jax coaxed. "I'm not trying to tell you what to do."

"Really? Because it sure as shit feels like you are. You have no idea what she put me through."

"I know enough."

"You know nothing."

He tried to grab the bottle out of my hand, but I chugged down another swig instead.

"I don't like seeing you like this, Kinley."

"Fine." I shrugged. "Then don't watch."

Before he could reply, I stomped away from him. I was angry that he was bringing her up when all I was trying to do was forget about the fact that she thought I'd want to speak to her, let alone see her. She meant nothing to me, and I was mostly pissed she was making Jax and me fight. Other than my aunt, he was the only person in my life I could count on.

I'd met him the first day of sixth grade which was also my first day at a new school, and I swear he could smell my fear. It was a reccurring joke between us. I was super shy back then, not used to having friends. When it came time to pick a partner in science class, I looked around the room in a panic, not knowing anyone.

Until a boy with kind eyes was hovering above my desk, asking me

However, rumors of our friendship were what school gossip was made of. Everyone thought we were hooking up behind closed doors, but it wasn't true. We weren't. It wasn't like that between us. We were just best friends. Jax was on the football team, and he'd been playing as the quarterback since he was six-years-old. My best friend was incredibly handsome and had absolutely no problem scoring with girls, on and off the field.

While I remained single, never having a boyfriend.

I didn't feel like I needed one. I had Jax, and that was good enough for me. He lived near my house, and since my aunt was constantly working in the ER as a registered nurse, Jax and I spent a lot of time together.

We slept in each other's beds more times than I could remember, which was probably why gossip ran rampant down our hallways. It wasn't a big deal. I was used to people talking about me once they knew I lived with my aunt and my mother wasn't in the picture.

Nobody knew why, though, and it only piqued their interest in wanting to continue to gossip about me. My aunt bought us a cute house in a nice neighborhood that reminded me of the movie Pleasantville. I learned pretty early on that everyone knew one another in this town. Complete opposite from the hustle and bustle of Cleveland where everyone kept to themselves.

When she decided to move us, she picked the first place her finger landed on the map. Lucky enough, the hospital in Fort Worth was looking for a new RN, and she filled the requirements, working all sorts of crazy hours, so I didn't see her a lot.

Yet another reason I was grateful for my friendship with Jax. He came from a broken home too. His parents got a divorce when he was younger, and neither one of them was around very much, so we found a family in one another.

Shoving away the thoughts, I chugged more booze while making my way deeper into the woods I wasn't familiar with. It was almost like I was walking into a different world. Tree after tree filled my surroundings as the woods came alive with the sounds of animals. When the smell of smoke and weed began fading, I realized how deep I truly was in the middle of nowhere.

"Shit," I whispered to myself, looking around. Hoping I'd find a sense of direction on where I'd come from. I must have gotten lost, ending up by a waterhole.

"Well, look what we have here," someone whispered from behind me, causing me to stumble back against a tree as he caged me in with his arms around the sides of my head. "I haven't seen you before. I'd remember such a pretty face and banging body," he rasped too close to my face, smelling like liquor and weed. "What's your name?"

I didn't recognize this guy, and the longer I stood there, the faster my heart began pounding against my chest. "Kinley," I replied, feeling much more vulnerable than before.

"Such a beautiful name, for such a beautiful girl. What are you doing all by yourself in the woods, babe? Don't you know you can run into a bear or a wolf?"

"Ummm … right. I need to go back." I sidestepped him to leave, but he blocked my advance.

"You don't need to leave. I'm here now."

My eyes widened. "I want to leave." I went to move again, but he wouldn't let me.

"Naw, I'm not done with you yet."

"Catch a clue—I'm not interested."

"I bet I can make you interested."

"If you don't let me leave, I'm going to scream."

He smiled. "I'll make you scream out alright, except it's going to be my name."

I turned my face as he leaned in to kiss me while the sound of another voice echoed through the woods, shouting, "Frank! Leave her the fuck alone! You're scaring her, you prick!"

I'd never been more relieved to hear a stranger's voice than I was at that moment. I released a deep breath I didn't realize I was holding when he backed away and spun around.

We both looked in the direction of where the voice had come from. There was a tall, stocky guy with dark hair standing a few feet away from us. I couldn't make out who he was yet. It was too dark out.

"Mind your own fucking business, Christian. This has nothing to do with you."

Christian? Was that Christian Troy?

Walking toward us, he grinned, looking in my direction before nodding to Frank. "You want to stay here with him?"

I peered back and forth between them, sputtering, "Umm … no."

Christian laughed, smirking wide.

It was Christian Troy. He was one of the most popular guys in our school. I couldn't help but smile back at him, feeling relieved he was there with me now. This was the first time he'd ever said a word to me. I didn't even think he knew I existed.

The reassuring expression on his face kept luring me in. When he caught me staring at his defined arms and broad chest, I blushed and looked back at Frank.

"Oh, I see," Frank chimed in. "You want to hang out with him instead? Is that it? Because I'll tell you right now, he doesn't do girlfriends."

Yeah, so I've heard.

Christian chuckled.

"I said that out loud, didn't I?"

He laughed again before nodding to Frank. "You can go now."

"Fuck you, man." With that, he spun and left, leaving Christian and me alone.

Now I was nervous for a whole different reason. I knew all I needed to know about him. His reputation preceded him wherever he went. It didn't matter what county we were in, everyone knew who Christian and his best friend Julian were. It had been that way since I'd moved here in middle school. Guys like them were all the same, every last one of them. Acting like they were hot shit and owned every place they walked into.

The worst part was that girls fed into their bullshit lines, cocky smirks, and zero fucks attitude. Through the years, I'd heard enough to know I needed to steer clear of Christian, and the fact that he was looking at me in the way guys did in romance movies was unsettling. As much as I didn't want him to have an effect on me, when one of the most popular boys in our school was devouring you with his gaze, you couldn't help but feel affected.

With an overconfident arched eyebrow, Christian narrowed his stare at me, and I swallowed hard. I watched as he continued making his way over to me, one assertive stride after the next.

Slowly, I licked my lips, my mouth suddenly becoming dry. Out of nowhere, it felt as though I was under some spell I couldn't control or begin to understand. His gaze immediately followed the movement of my tongue, and I found myself taking a step back while folding my arms over my chest and trying to stand my ground.

"Ummm … thanks," I expressed, wanting to break the awkward silence. "You kind of saved me just now."

"I do what I can. Kinley, right?"

"You know who I am?"

"Of course I know the name of one of the prettiest girls at our school."

My heart beat faster, and I couldn't help but notice how much he towered over me. He was tall, much taller than my five-foot-three frame. He was probably a little over six feet with dark hair and intense green eyes that had a hint of blue running through them. His chiseled jawline and facial hair only added to his sexy allure.

Not to mention he didn't look his age. He looked older. It was probably easy for him to buy booze or sneak into clubs which I knew he did with Julian. At least that was what everyone at our school gossiped.

Christian was unfazed, standing there in all his glory as I tried like hell to ignore his muscular build as he took me in.

"Are you checking me out?" I blurted, mentally chastising myself.

The one time I needed to sound calm and cool, and I couldn't pull it off. Not with the way he was staring at me.

"Would you like that?"

"No."

"That's not what your body's telling me."

"Well, you can't read my mind."

He gave me a sexy smirk, making my eyes roll.

"Fine. Try me."

"I don't want to embarrass you more than I already am."

"I'm not embarrassed," I shrieked, clearing my throat, my voice giving me away.

"Just remember you asked for it." He stepped toward me, leaving no room between us. "You're shocked that I know who you are, which is funny because I've actually asked around about you, but from what I've heard you're fucking your best friend."

I gasped. "I am not."

"You didn't let me finish. I don't think you're fucking Jax because you don't strike me as the kind of girl who spreads her legs for a guy who isn't solely fucking you, and Jax gets around."

He was right. I couldn't argue with him there.

"You don't date. You've never had a boyfriend. So that tells me you're either waiting for Prince Charming, or you have no interest in getting hurt. Which, let's face it, we're in high school, and the odds of a guy breaking your heart are very likely. Especially since you have no experience—"

"I have experience."

He smirked. "I bet you've never been kissed."

My mouth dropped open. "Yes, I have."

"Hmmm…" He thought about it for a second. "I call bullshit."

"I totally have."

"Alright. Then prove it."

I shrugged. "It was with this guy from another school."

"You mean the guy you just made up?"

"I'm not making him up. His name was Joseph, and he was the best kisser. We actually made out a lot. We couldn't get enough of each other."

"Right…"

"Stop with the snide comments. I'm not lying."

"Like I said, prove it."

"I just did. I told you his name was—"

"I said prove it, not make up lies."

"How am I supposed to prove it then?"

I never expected what came out of his mouth next. Never in a million years did I imagine one of the most popular guys in our school would challenge…

"You can prove it by letting me kiss you."

2

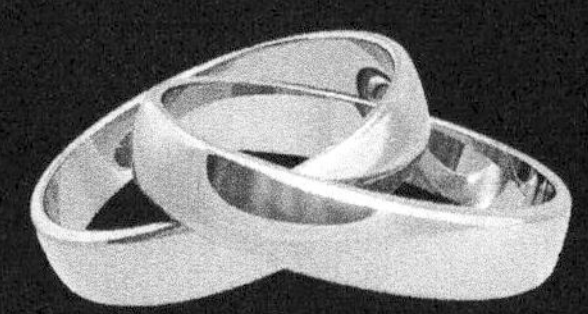

CHRISTIAN

"Are you for real?" she asked, completely caught off guard by my challenge.

I knew she was full of shit. I'd been asking around about Kinley McKenzie since middle school when she walked into my science class with a turquoise backpack. It was the first thing that caught my attention about her.

What girl in the sixth grade didn't have a pink or purple backpack? So naturally, I was instantly drawn to her, being that turquoise was my favorite color. I was going to ask her to be my science partner, but that fucker Jax beat me to it, and they'd been inseparable ever since. His head was so far up her ass, I was surprised he could still rail as many chicks as he did on a monthly basis. Supposedly, they weren't into each other.

Although I couldn't blame him if he was into her. She'd never been touched by anyone, and every guy at our school wanted to try to get with her just to say they were her first. On the other hand, I was drawn in by her ability to still smile despite all the shit she was going through with her mother.

I'd heard enough to know that her past wasn't anything that I'd experienced with my two loving parents, but I'd still been affected by my best friend Julian being dealt a shitty hand at life. Making both of us way too fast. The amount of times Julian had shown up at my house after being beaten by a foster parent was unreal.

To see the pain in his eyes, knowing he was trying to be strong for my parents who had to watch him go through so much bullshit because he was part of the system. They loved him like a second son, and my father being a lawyer had to get involved with the courts to constantly change his housing environment. Not that it mattered. He went from one shitty situation to the next. My parents wanted to adopt him, but Julian refused, saying they did enough for him.

My mom did the only thing she could. She made one of our guest bedrooms into his room, just so he'd feel like he had a home to come to when he needed it. I hated seeing all the shit he went through. He didn't deserve it. He was a good person, a great friend, someone I could count on no matter what. We were seven the first time Julian showed up at our house with a bloody nose from his foster dad.

At first, I didn't understand what had happened or why it was happening to him. By the time I was ten, I realized the severity of what he'd gone through, and I started having night terrors that he'd be beaten to death. I had to go to therapy. Julian didn't know that, though. My parents thought it was best, and for a while, it helped. My therapist said I was suffering from associated trauma, and it was normal to have the fears I was facing.

From that point forward, I made sure to do whatever I could to help my best friend. Fearing if I didn't, I'd lose him.

The sadness in Kinley's eyes mirrored Julian's even though she was smiling at me. It was like staring into my best friend's eyes, sparking this need inside of me to want to be there for her in any way I could. It was immediate, the desire to want to help her.

Protect her.

The second I saw her start walking into the woods alone, my feet moved on their own. I'd developed a protective quality to watch over those I loved, and there was a gravitational pull to protect Kinley at that moment. I was surprised Jax had left her alone long enough to get lost in the woods. He was by her side all the time. It was really fucking annoying, and since we were by ourselves for the first time since she'd walked into my science class all those years ago, I was going to use it to my advantage and kiss her.

Be her first kiss.

The longer we stood there, the more I craved to be in her life. It was the weirdest thing. I'd never experienced anything like it before. Maybe that was why I wanted to kiss her, knowing that to a girl like her…

It would mean something.

The truth was I was over it not meaning anything to me as well. There were only so many times I could hook up with a random chick. I was born and raised in this small ass town where everyone knew each other. I was almost sixteen, but felt much older. Wiser.

"Want to touch me?" I teased, smiling. "Make sure you're not dreaming?"

"So is this how it works?" she asked with amusement in her tone. "You save girls from assholes and then make your move?"

"Don't mind Frank. He's not much of a gentleman."

"And you are?"

"I mean, my mom did raise me right, and I have a little sister I need to protect."

"From guys like you?"

I placed my hand over my heart. "Ouch."

"Oh please … you don't fool me with your witty comebacks and amazing cheekbones. I know all about you too."

"Oh, so you've been asking around about me, Kinley?"

"Hardly, but everyone knows about you, Christian."

"I don't care what everyone knows. I want to know what you know."

"I know that you're one of the most popular guys at our school."

"Yeah, that doesn't mean shit to me."

"I find that hard to believe."

"Wow. You must think very highly of me?"

"I don't think anything about you."

I touched my heart again, looking down at my hand. "Am I bleeding? Or do you want to dig that dagger a little deeper?"

She giggled in that girly way that usually annoyed me, but coming from her it didn't. It was cute.

"So what else do you know?"

"That you're with a lot of girls."

"Oh, so you know that my dick is huge?"

Her eyes went wide. "Not as big as your ego!"

I laughed, I couldn't help it. She was fucking adorable. "How much longer do you plan on stalling? You could just say I'm right and you're a liar, and then you wouldn't have to pretend like you're unaffected by my awesome personality."

"I'm not stalling." She shook her head. "I just don't have to prove anything to you either."

"You're the one who said I didn't know what you were thinking, and I just proved to you that I do. Like right now, you're thinking how much you want me to kiss you, but you're worried I'm going to know that it's your first kiss by the way your lips move with mine, so I'll ease your mind since I'm a gentleman, and tell you that all you have to do is follow my lead. I'll do all the work." I winked. "You're welcome."

"Ugh! You're unbelievable. You know that?"

"Oh, I know. I'm especially unbelievable at kissing, which you're about to find out for yourself, Kins."

"Kins? You have a nickname for me now?"

"Would you prefer I call you sweetness?"

She arched an eyebrow. "Sweetness?"

"Yeah, I know you're going to taste as sweet as you look."

"Dude! You just have a witty comeback for everything, huh?"

"What can I say, pretty girl? You bring out the best in me."

She smiled, a real smile that time as she tucked her hair behind her ear. I instantly reached over and pulled it out to tug on the ends of it, letting my fingertips graze her cheek.

"Is this one of your moves?"

"Do you want it to be?"

"I have no interest in being another one of your girls."

I grinned. "Jealous?"

"You wish. I'm not one of your cheerleaders."

With a hard edge, I replied, "That you aren't."

"Why do you want to kiss me anyway?"

"Can't a friend just help out another friend?"

"We're friends now? When did that happen? I don't even like you."

Calling her bluff, I narrowed my eyes at her. "That really hurts, Kins."

"You're so full of it."

"And you're beautiful."

"I don't know if I should be offended or flattered that you're hitting on me."

"If I had to choose, I'd prefer the latter."

"Well then, thank God you don't."

"That sassy little mouth of yours is really fucking cute."

She was gorgeous. The girl didn't even have to try. She was naturally stunning. I just stood there in awe of her. There was something about the way she was looking at me that truly had my mind reeling with what her lips would feel like against mine.

"I guess letting you kiss me could be like a thank you for saving me."

"I didn't save you. I protected you."

"What's the difference?"

"You don't need saving, Kinley. You're a survivor all on your own."

Her face paled, understanding I knew more than she assumed I would. I didn't know what was worse. Her pretending like she didn't want me to kiss her, or her wanting me to. I couldn't help noticing the look in her eyes. They spoke volumes, roping me in, taking hold of my mind, and not letting go. I was so fucking conflicted. The effect she was having on me, and we'd only just spoken for the first time.

What was happening?

As if reading my mind, she changed the subject. "Frank's going to talk shit. You know that, right?"

"Good. Let him run his mouth. It will keep other fuckers away from you too."

"But not you?"

Unable to hold back any longer, I coaxed, "I'm going to kiss you now, Kinley."

I waited a couple of seconds for her to object, and when she didn't, I leaned forward, closing the small distance between us. Wanting to touch her skin, my hands reached up and grabbed ahold of her cheeks. The smell of her assaulted my senses as I softly claimed her lips, laying my mouth right on hers. Her eyes tightly shut, her breathing hitched, and her arms fell to her sides. Right from the start, I could tell she had no idea what she was doing.

Her lips were smooth against mine, and I could feel her heart drumming so fucking fast against my chest. The desire to ruin her for every other guy was as real as the feelings I was experiencing toward her.

Slowly, I parted my lips, pulling her in closer, and she followed my lead, matching the same rhythm I'd set. My tongue touched her lips before she did the same, leaving the craziest sensation in her wake. I pulled back my tongue, and she understood what I wanted, what I sought. She gently slid hers into my eager mouth.

My tongue did the same as hers, turning this kiss into something more than I thought it would be.

I was losing myself in her.

From her lips to her eyes, to the sounds she was making.

Words couldn't describe what was happening at that moment between us. The feelings she stirred with each stroke of our tongues. Feelings I didn't think were possible to experience. That I didn't even think existed.

I didn't want to stop kissing her.

It was surreal.

Consuming.

And I wanted more.

When another soft moan escaped her mouth, I pecked her lips one last time before gradually pulling away. Already missing her touch. Incoherent thoughts ran rapidly through my mind.

I was grinning down at her as her eyes fluttered open, not removing my hands from the sides of her face. My infatuated stare hadn't changed—if anything it was worse.

Murmuring against her lips, I rasped, "Like I said, you've never been kissed until now. Until me."

Her chest was rising and falling, as she waited for what I would say next. Surprising us both when I added…

"What other first of yours can I have next?"

3

Kinley

Now

It had been six months since Julian and Autumn's wedding, and I couldn't believe how fast time was slipping by. I felt awful for ruining their wedding, even though they claimed we didn't.

Christian and I didn't know they were in the barn and overheard our fight. The embarrassment I felt when they confronted us seconds after Christian kissed me was an emotion that still lingered in my mind.

"Oh my God! You guys are getting a divorce?" Autumn exclaimed, rushing toward us.

Our shocked expressions snapped to her worried gaze with Julian right behind her. He was calmer and more collected which didn't surprise me. They'd spent years hooking up behind everyone's back, including her brother's, until Julian had to leave town. He couldn't continue to lie to a family that had taken him in as if he were their own.

Ten years later, they made their way back to each other, and now they were married. Their special day was now ruined because of us, making me feel horrible that this was what they would remember in the years to come.

"Guys, please go back to your reception. We can talk about this lat-

er," I reasoned, hoping they'd listen.

"No, we can talk about this now," Autumn persisted. "How long has this been going on?"

"Long enough to know we're not right for each other anymore." I looked at Christian for support on this, but it was evident by his composure he wasn't going to give me an inch.

"What are you talking about? That's impossible. You've been together for twenty years."

"Autumn, there's a lot you don't know."

Julian grabbed her arm. "Kid, let them be."

"Christian, do Mom and Dad know?"

He shook his head, and I answered for him, "We're going to tell them."

"When?"

"Soon," was all I could reply.

Julian pulled her away. "Come on, let's get back to our guests." I'd never been more grateful for him than I was right then.

Autumn gazed at us hesitantly before she reluctantly listened to her husband. After they were gone, I glared back at Christian.

"Thanks for nothing," I bit. "You could have helped me, you know? Is this how it's going to be when we tell your parents?"

"You need to remember that you're the one who wants this divorce, Kinley. And don't you ever forget that."

He turned and followed them back to the reception while I stayed there for another few minutes, thinking about the mess our lives had become.

Two weeks later, we were sitting at their table for dinner when Christian took it upon himself to announce our divorce to them without discussing it with me first. Completely blindsiding me, and I knew he did it to be spiteful.

Announcing, "You guys can stop pretending like you don't know we're getting a divorce. I'm sure Autumn already told you."

They'd just gotten back from their honeymoon in St. Bart's, and this was the last thing we needed to discuss.

"Christian," Autumn coaxed. "What was I supposed to do? Huh? They have a right to know."

I sighed, intervening, "Please don't argue because of us."

"So then, it's true?" his mom asked, making me bow my head. The shame immediately eating me alive.

For the next hour, we had to hear his parents talk about the ups and downs of marriage, and how important it was to stay connected, like we didn't already know that. They were adamant we could work through it, and we'd come out stronger in the end.

I never thought we'd be in this situation to begin with, and it wasn't like I had fallen out of love with him. He was still my everything, but we weren't on the same page anymore. We'd drifted apart, becoming two different people instead of a couple. We weren't even on the same wavelength anymore.

Arguing with him at therapy only added to the conviction I felt about ending our marriage. We couldn't go on like this. It wasn't fair to either of us, and for the life of me, I didn't understand why he couldn't see that.

"Christian, that's not fair!" I shouted, staring him down at our therapist's office.

"What's not fair, Kinley? Because the only thing not fucking fair is the fact that you're making us get a divorce!"

"I'm not making us get a divorce! You want one too! You just can't bring yourself to say the words, so I'm doing it for the both of us!"

"Oh, that's fucking rich. You know everything, don't you?"

"Oh, please! You want to talk about egos? Yours is so fucking big I'm surprised you're able to walk past the doors of our therapist's office!"

"Kinley, Christian…"

"What?!" we both yelled in unison, glaring at our marriage counselor.

This poor woman.

The number of times she had to play mediator between us in the last year was not lost on me. I swear it was the only thing she did, constantly having to interfere with our dragged-out fights. I couldn't remember the last time Christian and I weren't screaming at each other.

"We've talked about this before. You need to learn to use your feeling words. Shouting at one another isn't going to solve anything."

"There's nothing to solve according to my wife, Dr. Webb. We're signing divorce papers in a few days, remember?"

"I know, but in the meantime, you can still try to express yourselves in a positive way."

I glanced at him, trying to listen to her and do my best at leveling out my tone. "Christian, when you say things like I want a divorce and you don't, it really upsets me. I know deep down you're deflecting and placing blame on me when we both know we haven't been happy in a very long time."

With a condescending expression on his face, he replied, "Kinley… I don't want to upset you, but when you say I want a divorce too, it's complete and utter bullshit." He sarcastically smiled, looking back at our therapist. "I don't have a feeling word for bullshit other than what it is which is fucking bullshit."

"Do you see, Dr. Webb?" I pointed at him. "Do you see what I have to deal with? He's an asshole!"

"Kinley," she said in that soothing voice I hated.

"Right." I nodded, trying to once again control my tone. "He's patronizing me, and it makes him look like an arrogant know-it-all, and it makes me feel like a child instead of his wife."

"Patronizing you?" he disputed. "Because I don't want a divorce, I'm an asshole? Well, since you want one, Kins, what does that make you? 'Cause I can think of a lot of words that are comparable to arrogant and know-it-all, and one that specifically stands out right now would definitely be selfish."

"Selfish?" I narrowed my heated stare at him. "Are you for real? I'm the furthest thing from selfish, Christian. Like always, you're not hearing me!"

"Oh, that's right! You're always right, and I'm always wrong. You're just perfect, and everything is all my fault."

"I didn't say that! See? You never listen to me, and that's our biggest problem. You hear what you want to and it's why nothing ever gets solved between us."

"You can't let go of anything. You hold onto everything, and it builds and builds until all you do is nag me when you could have just said something to me when it was actually bothering you."

"When am I supposed to tell you? You're never around. You work all the time! It's either you're at the office with your patients, or you're at the hospital delivering their babies! You're there more than you are at home, so when am I supposed to talk to you, Christian? Because I don't fucking know anymore. Do I need to make an appointment with your secretary, or do I need to talk to your RN since you spend more time with her than you do with me? How's that supposed to make me feel?"

"For fuck's sake! We're back to this bullshit again? I work for you! I work because your life has been hard, and I want to make it easier for you. In the same way I have for the last twenty years. I work to give you everything you've ever wanted. I work for your big, beautiful house, and your six-figure car, for your designer clothes, and fuck-me heels! For your hair appointments, for your nails, for your lunches with your girlfriends, for the food that's on the damn table every single night! I work to make your life better! Now what the hell do you do for me?"

I gasped. "I work too, but you don't see me revolving my life around my career!"

"You're an English professor, and I'm an OB/GYN—it's a little different, don't you think?"

"Oh! Here you go again! Your career is more important than mine."

"I didn't say that. Once again, you're just putting words in my mouth."

"How many times do I have to tell you that I would much rather have you than any of those things?"

"Bull-fucking-shit! You love the life I've made for you. I have given you everything! Everything, Kinley! And you can't even give me the one thing I want from you!"

I shook my head. "I knew you blamed me."

"If you would have listened to me in the first place, we wouldn't be in this situation, and we would have the family we both want."

"Christian," Dr. Webb interrupted. "We've talked about this. You're placing unnecessary blame on Kinley. She couldn't have known what would happen that night."

"You're right. I'm just..." He took a deep breath before his eyes connected with mine. "I'm sorry, Kinley. I didn't mean it."

"Here's where we differ yet again, Christian. I know you meant what you just said, and if I could go back and change things, don't you think I would? I'd give anything to take back that night, but I can't keep beating myself up about it. I've done it for over ten years, and I have to let it go. I have to let you go too. It's the only thing I can do to make things right."

"That doesn't make anything right," he expressed. "It only makes it worse. All I want is for us to be together, but I'm exhausted fighting for us when you don't give a shit."

"That's not fair!"

"Nothing about this is fair! Especially this divorce that only you want. I still see us. We're still here, Kinley. I don't know how you can't see it."

"We can't stay together because sometimes we see a glimpse of what and who we used to be. That's not a marriage, Christian."

All the wind from my sails deflated when he added, "A marriage is up and down, it's good and bad, it's for better or for worse, that's a fucking marriage."

—Christian—

I didn't know what else I could do, what else I could say, I was at my wit's end. There was no getting through to her. She was hell bent on ending us, and I couldn't for the life of me figure out why we couldn't work through this.

There once was a time we thought we could get through anything life threw at us.

We made it through our sad stories…

But could we make it through our last?

Then

A month had passed since I'd last spoke to Christian, and I'd be lying if I said he didn't consume my thoughts. Every time I licked or touched my lips, I remembered the feel of his against mine. The sensation of his tongue lingered in my mouth, especially when I was asleep. I started to dream about him, recalling his last words to me before I walked away that night.

"What other first of yours can I have next?"

By the sincere expression on his face, I knew he was being serious, and it scared me more than anything. I never cared to have a boyfriend, yet I couldn't stop thinking about what might happen between us if he continued to pursue me.

But he didn't.

I hadn't seen or heard from him since the first time we talked in the woods and he became my first kiss. It was summer vacation, though, and he didn't know where I lived or the places I hung out at. We ran in different crowds. Or maybe that was just me making excuses for him.

If he liked me, he'd find a way to reach out, right?

Ugh! This was so confusing. I didn't want to be that girl. The one who waited around for the guy to call, the one who cried when he didn't, the one who surrounded her life and thoughts solely about him. I hated that girl. She was weak, and I was not frail. It was why I never wanted to be in a relationship to begin with. It was safer that way.

My heart was already shattered by the woman who was supposed to love me the most.

Then why couldn't I stop thinking about him?

"I think there's a spot open over there," I told Jax, bringing my thoughts back to the present and not lost in my own mind over a boy I hadn't heard from.

Pointing to the only available parking spot on the grass for the party we were attending, I smiled as he pulled into the space. The empty land by James' house turned into our private parking lot, and it looked like a small car dealership with all the cars parked and ready to go have a great time. It was Saturday night, and James was having one of his infamous parties at his parents' house. They were out of town, and anytime they weren't around he used it to his advantage and threw a huge party.

His dad did something with international real estate, and at one point he was having an affair with his assistant which meant his mom now traveled with him. These were the downfalls of living in a small town—

everyone knew everyone else's business, and gossip spread like wildfire. I tried not to pay attention to it, but it was hard to ignore when everyone's dirty laundry was aired out in the open for all of us to see.

I was honestly surprised more people didn't know about my toxic past, but I did a great job at pretending as if I didn't have one.

James' place was huge, and the best part of it was its location. A private waterfront property on Eagle Mountain Lake where there was so much distance between the houses the cops were never called on us for disturbing the peace. It was the perfect place to let loose and not have to worry about getting in trouble for underage drinking and the obscene amount of weed in the air.

His parents never found out, or maybe they just didn't give a shit. Everyone partied near the lake where country music blared through the expensive speaker system. Later in the night, the party would move into the house, and people would start hooking up. The bedrooms of his home had seen more action than a porno flick, and I couldn't help but wonder how many times Christian had used one of those rooms.

It was almost seven by the time Jax parked his Jeep, and I was already counting down the minutes until I could go home and curl up with the book I was currently reading. I loved to read. It was my escape for many years when I desperately needed one, not wanting to live in the reality of my dysfunctional ass home.

If you could even call it a home. Trust me, it was far from any home you'd ever want to live in. My mother made sure of it. I never stayed long at these parties like Jax did, and I only showed up since he wouldn't let me stay home on a Saturday night. I'd wait until he found some random chick for the evening, telling him this was my cue to dip out.

Sometimes he'd put up an argument and I'd have to stay, but most of the time I called an Uber with no problems. He'd always walk outside with me to get a photo of the license plate, making sure I was okay. He was a great friend like that.

Time just sort of seemed to fly by at these parties. Before I knew it, I had been there for a few hours, drinking and hanging out with Jax before a girl with a short skirt caught his attention.

"I see you eye-fucking her, Jax. You can leave me now."

He smiled. "You sure?"

"Of course. I mean, when was the last time you got laid? What, a week ago? That's like a lifetime for you."

"Cute, Kinley." He laughed. "You going to head home?"

"Yeah."

"Text me when your Uber gets here, alright?"

"You know I can just take a picture of the license plate and text it to you?"

"But then I don't get to say goodbye to my favorite girl."

"Yeah, yeah, yeah. Save your lines for your next hussy."

"So," the chick purred, suddenly standing behind him. "Is it my turn to have a chance with the infamous Jax Colton? I've been told about you and your skills. When am I going to get a turn to show you mine?"

I rolled my eyes, and he smiled wide.

"You're quite the ladies' man, and I want to see what all the fuss is about." She raised her eyebrows. "Oh, I'm sorry. Is this your girlfriend?"

"No. I'm his best friend, and you can take him. I'm used to it."

"Kinley," Jax exclaimed, winking at me.

She sucked in her lower lip and narrowed her eyes, allowing them to wander down his body. With her mousy face, perfect boobs, and big ass, she was right up his alley.

"I'll text you a picture, Jax. Go show her your moves, Casanova."

He extended his arm and she followed suit, linking her fingers through his.

"Text me when you get home too."

I nodded, watching as they walked hand-in-hand inside of James' house. Instead of getting an Uber, I decided to make my way down to the lake. The water was stunning this time of year with the bright stars in the sky. I found a secluded spot behind some trees and leaned against one, getting lost in the beauty of the night.

I could still hear a bit of the music coming from the speakers, and I closed my eyes. Taking a deep breath in and out, my mind began drifting which was never a good thing.

The song and lake dragged me back to another place and time where my life consisted of trying to find my mother yet again.

"Mom!" I shouted into the wind, hoping she'd hear over the loud music they were playing from a car I didn't recognize. Once I was at the bottom of the hill, I saw all the empty bottles of liquor and beer. Shaking my head, I stared deep into her hazy, drunk gaze. "I've been looking for you for hours! What are you doing?" I finally found her down by the lake near our house. It wasn't usually one of her spots to get shitfaced.

"Kinley! Baby!" she called out when she saw me rushing toward her. "Come dance!"

"Where's your clothes, Mom?"

"Is this your daughter?" some man I'd never seen before questioned, pissing me off further. This must have been his idea.

"Yes! Isn't she stunning?! My beautiful baby!"

I grabbed her jeans and shirt off the ground—she was only wearing her bra and panties. "Mom, you're going to get arrested again if you don't—"

"You're such a party pooper! We were just swimming! Come swimming with us!"

It was only then I noticed her guy for the night wasn't wearing anything but his boxers. Shoving her clothes onto her chest, I demanded, "Mom, let's go."

"No! I'm having fun. You go. I'll be home later."

"No, you'll be home now. You can't—"

"I'm the adult, Kinley. You can't boss me around."

"Then act like one for once!"

"Your kid is a drag," the random man chimed in. "I'm outta here."

"Good! Fucking leave! You have no business with her! Did you know she's on parole—"

She pushed me hard, and I stumbled back, losing my footing.

"Fuck you, Kinley! Get outta here! You're the one who has no business being here!"

I wasn't surprised by her harsh words. This wasn't the first or last time she'd made me look for her. I hated when she got like this. It was hard enough to get through to her when she wasn't drinking. Alcohol added to the endless problem that was my mother.

"Mom, are you taking your meds—"

Before I could finish my sentence, she backhanded me across the face so hard I instantly saw stars. I wish I could tell you this was the first time she'd laid her hands on me, but it wasn't. Most of the time, she'd forget she'd hit me at all.

My hand immediately went to my face, feeling the sting of her ring against my cheek. I looked down at my hand, seeing blood, and it was only then she realized what she had just done.

Slowly, she backed away from me with wide eyes. "Kinley, I'm so sor—"

"You alright, sweetness?"

My stare shot up, locking eyes with the guy I least expected. Once again he'd saved me, except this time it was from my memories.

—Christian—

There was something about the way she was sitting against the tree with her eyes shut and her hair blowing in the wind that truly took my breath away. Which had never happened before, me taking an interest in someone outside of my family and friends, especially a girl I'd only had one conversation with. Yet there I was, completely mesmerized by the vision sitting in front of me as if she appeared out of thin air.

My attraction to her was as strong as it was the night I'd first kissed her.

Every day since I thought about her—what she was doing, how she was feeling, when I would see her again. The questions were never-ending, so was the desire to feel her mouth against mine again.

She was like this mythical creature luring me toward her. From the moment I saw her walk down here alone, there was no choice to be made. I followed her, gravitating toward her in the same way I did that night in the woods. Before I knew what was happening, I was watching a memory play out in her mind. Knowing whatever she was remembering wasn't pleasant, I could tell by her face.

She was crying. Her expression showed nothing but pain, and I found myself hurting right along with her. It didn't make any sense, the immediate connection I felt toward her. All I knew was I wanted to make her smile and laugh.

Over the years, I did exactly that.

Until one day, it was the opposite.

And all I did was make her cry.

5

CHRISTIAN

I wanted to make it better.

I wanted to make *her* better.

"You alright, sweetness?"

Her gaze went wide when she realized I'd caught her crying, and she immediately wiped away her tears, camouflaging her distress before reason settled in. Quickly standing, she was about to leave, but I grabbed her wrist, stopping her, and for some unknown reason, she let me.

"Don't go," was all I could say.

I didn't know it then, but those two words changed the course of our lives and fused us together.

She didn't reply. However, her cautious stare was still locked with mine. Neither one of us was able to look away from each other. It was evident my attraction to her was very much reciprocated. Our stares mirrored one another while more questions plagued our minds. I wanted to know everything about her.

The good.

The bad.

The ugly.

I knew there wasn't a lot of good in her past. Maybe not even in her present. Her future, though, I could make that good, and I knew that when

I was only sixteen-years-old.

"What's wrong?" I finally asked with sincerity laced in my tone. I didn't want to scare her away, but I had to know. I had to fix it.

I had to fix her.

"Mind your own business, Christian." Her voice was an equal mixture of anger and sadness as her face frowned, almost like she regretted what she'd just replied. Allowing her memories to speak for themselves.

Her response stung, but it didn't shock me. We were strangers, and she barely knew me. She'd only heard awful things about me. I couldn't blame her for not wanting to open up. If anything, I was happy her first instinct was to protect herself.

Her wall was so tall and thick, and all I wanted to do was break through her icy demeanor.

I wanted her to let me in. If only for a second, I'd take it.

"I'm making it my business, Kinley, but I'll settle for a smile instead."

She narrowed her eyes at me, and I took the opportunity to sit in the same spot she'd just stood from. Waiting for I didn't know what.

I did the only thing I could in a moment that felt bigger than us.

I spoke from the heart. "You know we all have sad stories," I shared, catching myself off guard. I'd never opened up to anyone, but she wasn't just anyone, and I knew that then. "The first time I realized bad things happen to good people, I was seven." Outside of my parents and therapist, I'd never admitted that to anyone. "The first time I grasped that I couldn't do anything but pray for those bad things to go away, I was eight."

I felt her take a seat beside me, fully aware she was hanging onto my every word. I swallowed hard, never feeling as vulnerable as I did then.

"The first time I understood that prayer wasn't enough to make those bad things go away, I was nine." I glanced over at her, needing to look into her eyes.

The concern for me was written clear across her face. She, more than anyone, understood what I was admitting.

"Now the first time I sat in a therapist's office, telling my doctor I was terrified those bad things were going to take away my best friend, I was ten."

She jerked back. "Julian?"

I nodded.

"I had no idea."

"Yeah, nobody does."

"But he's okay now, right?"

I shook my head. "I don't know if he'll ever really be okay. The shit he's seen and been through is what nightmares are made of, and it doesn't just go away. It stays with you and becomes a part of you, and if you let it, it'll consume you."

"I'm so sorry, Christian. I can't imagine how hard it was for you to see your best friend in pain. Sometimes I think that's worse, you know? Seeing the ones we love the most hurting and not being able to stop it. No matter how hard you try, how much you cry and fight for them, in the end, all you're doing is slowly dying right along with them." She paused, letting her words sink in. "Is there anything I can do?"

"Yeah. You can do something for me."

"What's that?"

I didn't hold back, speaking with conviction, "You can tell me your sad story."

—Kinley—

I walked down to that lake to be alone.

With my thoughts.

My memories.

My trauma.

As much as I hated to admit it, I missed my mom. The sight of her, the smell of her, the sound of her voice, the feel of her warmth, her sadness, her happiness, her love…

Even her hate.

The familiarity of it all.

It was comforting when it was supposed to have been afflicting.

I thought about his request before shaking my head. "I wouldn't even know where to start."

"The beginning, Kinley. I want you to tell me everything."

I stared into his eyes, feeling like we were on the same side. Both of us knew what it was like to pray and not feel heard. In the blink of an eye, my life changed overnight, and I was no longer living under the same roof as the woman who was supposed to be my mother but acted more like the drunk she was.

I shut my eyes, recalling the last time I saw her.

"Please!" she yelled loud enough to break glass. "Please don't take her from me! She's all I have! She's all I fucking have!"

"Ugh!" I grabbed my head in between my hands.

Those were the last words I heard her say as child services dragged me out of our Section 8. Day in and day out, I lived and breathed her demons until one day I was set free, but I still felt like a caged bird. There was no running away from my memories.

Not then.

Not now.

I hadn't realized I'd begun crying, tears spilling out over what I could never change. It didn't matter how much I'd tried, how much I'd cried, nothing ever changed.

Not with her.

Not with us.

I might have been her daughter, but she was not my mother, not in the ways that counted.

A wave of emotions took over, and when Christian grabbed my wrist to stop me from leaving and took a seat where I had once sat, I couldn't have left even if I'd wanted to.

And the truth was, I didn't want to.

I listened to him with the same longing I had for my mom. The same thoughts, the same fears, the same realizations of what I shouldn't have experienced at such a young age. The sincerity in his tone had caught me off guard, making me feel like I was the only person he had ever shared these confessions with other than his therapist and family.

Not even Julian.

For the first time in my life, I didn't feel so alone. He understood what I went through on a daily basis, and it overwhelmed me as much as it calmed me. I was seeing a side to him he didn't show anyone, and I had no idea why…

All I knew was that I didn't want it to go away.

I didn't want him to go away.

As soon as I felt the back of his fingers wipe away my tears, we once again locked eyes. Something deep inside of me told me I could trust him, but the intensity of what we were experiencing toward each other wasn't anything I'd ever experienced with anyone before.

It was thrilling.

Terrifying.

It was everything and more.

I was the first to break eye contact between us, looking back toward the lake instead and trying to reel in my emotions that never went away. I contemplated if I was really going to do this. I could feel his gaze on the side of my face, burning a hole into my skin, and a part of me knew he sensed that.

The effect he had on me.

I gazed up at the sky, needing a minute to gather my thoughts and what was happening between us. The stars shined bright above our heads, illuminating against the darkness of the sky with the moon smiling high like a Cheshire cat. The lake breeze brought a slight chill to the air, and I hugged my knees to my chest in a reassuring gesture, shielding myself to create some warmth around me.

I sat there beside him, feeling his honesty, his support…

His love?

Taking a deep breath, I opened my mouth and murmured, "This isn't the first time she's lost custody of me," just loud enough for him to hear. My eyebrows rose, surprised with my own revelation. I finally admitted a truth out loud, and it felt fucking amazing. "They say people can't remember memories before the age of six, but I remember it clear as day. Like it only just happened yesterday. My mom left me in our piece of shit car when I was only four-years-old. I can still taste my tears, I can still hear my screams, and I can still feel the sweat pouring down my face and body." I hesitated for a moment, reliving the past for what felt like the hundredth time.

"By the time our neighbor found me, I'd passed out from heat exhaustion. I remember waking up in the hospital with all these strangers around me, begging for my mom to come and rescue me." I wiped away the tears that were now streaming down my face, one right after the other. "How fucking ironic, right? She was the only reason I was there to begin with, and I still only wanted her. For years I only wanted her, until I realized that she never really wanted me." I covered my face, desperately trying to hide from him.

He didn't allow it. He pulled down my hands, and I turned my face, not wanting him to see right through me.

"I remember her running into the hospital, rushing toward me, and before she could comfort me in her arms, the cops grabbed her and threw her face-down onto the ground. She screamed … she screamed so fucking loud for me that sometimes I can still hear her in my sleep. My whole world was constantly ripped apart, yet I still loved her. I still prayed for her. I still yearned for her. I still wanted my mom more than anything in this world."

I couldn't stop the tears that fell out of my eyes, and I didn't want to. I earned them, every last one—they were my badge of honor.

"I was in and out of foster homes until she served her time and got custody of me again. Promising me that things were going to be different, that she was clean, she was taking her meds, she was happy… And for a while she was. My mom could have the highest of highs, but then the lowest of lows—there was no middle ground with her. She was up, or she was down. She was manic, or she was calm."

"Your mom's bipolar."

We locked eyes again.

"That's just the tip of the iceberg. My mother is a lot of things, but being a mother is not one of them. At first, I believed her. Even when I knew better, I still believed her. The woman who ripped my life to shreds day after day was the same one I prayed would tuck me into bed at night."

My chest heaved, and my heart broke while Christian's stare never faltered. He sat there patiently listening to every word out of my mouth, never once interrupting me. I instantly looked down when I felt him gently place his hand on top of mine in the grass before he laced them together. It was such a soothing, reassuring gesture. Feeling like we were one.

To have a real connection with someone, with a boy who didn't even know me, but wanted to know everything was an emotion I'd never experienced before.

I wanted to tell him everything, especially the effect he was having on me, and for a second, I'd thought about it. Except, I realized I didn't have to, he knew—he was feeling our deep connection too.

Making it a little easier to continue, "I was by myself a lot. I'm still by myself a lot. More than I should be at my age. My aunt works at the hospital all the time, and she's barely around. All I have is Jax. I think I'd be lost without him. Sometimes I think it's easier for my aunt to work and not have to look at me. I remind her of my mother, her sister, and the shit she put her through was similar to what she did to me. She didn't know she had a daughter. My mom ran away from home when she was fifteen and never looked back. You know what they say, the apple doesn't fall far from the tree. Her mother was the same way. I come from a long line of crazy women." I laughed, even though I hated that fact.

"I don't want to be like them. I'll never be like them. I refuse. The only thing my mom has ever done for me was to have her court-appointed lawyer find her sister. He did, and she came to my rescue before I was awarded to the state."

My eyes were fixated on his hand that never left mine. In the dark, his rough, calloused fingers were so comforting resting over mine, and I wanted to turn my hand over to feel him.

When he reached over and lightly grazed the side of my cheek with his other hand, his fingers moved to tug on the ends of my hair that framed my face. His knuckles grazed my cheek, and I nervously licked my lips, peeking up at him through my lashes.

"It wasn't you, Kinley. She's just sick."

"I know. She self-medicated with whatever she could get her hands on—it was mostly booze. I slept on couch cushions for most of my life, and we were in and out of shelters. Sometimes we lived out of her piece of shit car. As a little girl, she made a game out of it. How many people could we get money from standing at an intersection? The older I got, the more I didn't want to play her games. I haven't spoken to or seen her in three and a half years. She wants to see me, and a little part of me wants to see her too." My face frowned. "That's normal, right? Or am I just really stupid?"

"It's not stupid." Slowly, he kissed away my tears until his lips were near my mouth.

It was the craziest sensation in all my life. He kissed me again. Except for this time…

It felt like we were breathing each other in.

6

CHRISTIAN

Now

I walked into the house that used to be our home with boxes in my hands. Today was the day I was officially moving out. Everything was ironed out with our lawyers. I was giving Kinley the house and her car. We were splitting our savings, and selling our two vacation homes—one was in St. Thomas, and the other was in Colorado. Since we didn't have any kids, our settlement was simple.

In three days, we'd sign our divorce papers, and then our attorneys would schedule our day in court for the judge to sign off and make it official.

We were no longer married.

Our last therapy session was two days ago, and nothing was sorted or fixed between us, not one damn thing. We hadn't spoken which was by far the worst silence, when we were deliberately not wanting to speak to each other, it was worse than when we were arguing. At least then it felt as if we were fighting for something.

However, at this point, I didn't know what to say, what to feel, fuck…

For the last few weeks I'd been staying at Julian and Autumn's ranch, needing to get out of this house and all the memories it held. I couldn't keep up with the turmoil of it all, and I still had a business to run and patients to see.

I'd lost…

Our marriage.

Our love.

Her.

I'd lost everything that ever mattered to me, and it felt like my life was falling apart and spinning out of control. I couldn't take it anymore, not my thoughts, or my questions, or my fucking patience. For years I'd prayed this was just a phase, another chapter in our lives, something we would work through and tell our kids about one day.

I was wrong.

Now I was facing our failures head-on. With a hole in my heart, I walked around our house that she'd made into a home. Remembering every moment we'd shared inside these painted walls.

From the first to the last, they played out in front of me. Everywhere I looked there was a memory or milestone we'd been through together.

"What do you think?" Kinley pointed to the three paint swatches on the wall in the living room. "Which color?"

"They all look the same to me."

"Christian, those are three very distinctive colors."

"They're all white, Kins."

"One is white, the other is off white, and that one is satin white. Can you see the difference now?"

I shook my head, laughing. "No."

She teased, "Are you color blind?"

I smiled, tugging her toward me. "The only thing I'm blind for is you, sweetness."

My fingers slid along the island in our kitchen, recalling the first time we stood there after closing on our house. We were so happy, so in love, so fucking consumed with one another.

I gripped onto her ass and lifted her up onto the island. Spreading her legs, I slipped in between them to kiss her neck.

"Christian!" she giggled. "I need to put the groceries away, and then I have to cook dinner."

"The only thing I'm hungry for is you."

She giggled again, making my cock twitch at the sound.

"We're not going to have anything to eat!"

"Baby..." I kissed my way down her perfect body until I was on my knees in front of her, sliding down her panties. "I'm ready to eat now."

She laughed, throwing her head back. It was one of my favorite sounds. As soon as she felt my tongue on her clit, she loudly moaned, and I ate what I wanted for dinner.

Step by step, I made my way through our home.

Hearing her laughs.

Seeing her smiles.

Feeling our love.

Starting from the front door where I carried her over the threshold, to the stairs where I made love to her for hours on end, to the travertine floors we'd spent entirely too much time at Lowe's for. Every corner of this house held a memory of our life together.

There was no escaping it…

The good.

The bad.

"Christian!" she shouted. "You're not listening to me!"

"How can I when all you do is yell at me? For fuck's sake! I just walked in from a fourteen-hour work day, and you greet me with nothing but your bullshit!"

"It's the only time I have before you go hurrying back to the hospital again to deliver another baby!"

"Well, at least someone is having babies around here!"

Over the years, we both said things we didn't mean. Letting our anger speak for itself was never a good thing. It was one of the reasons we tried therapy, thinking it might help, it might repair what was broken between us. Or, at least help us talk to each other without screaming.

At first, I thought it was working until our problems became bigger than our love. Somewhere along the way, we lost respect for one another, and anything was free game when it came down to hurting each other.

Words had the power to cut you, and we'd been using our tongues as butcher knives for the last few years.

It wasn't always like this. We were even featured in Home and Gardens—the successful doctor and his beautiful professor wife. A lot of time and devotion was put into every detail of this house, down to the pillows on the sofas, and the accessories she perfectly matched to the tones of the room. I had no part in that—it was all Kinley.

Saying it was the first home she'd ever had.

"Oh! You can't use that throw blanket, Christian. It's only for decoration."

I grinned. "You bought a blanket we can't use?"

She smiled. "But look how nice it looks."

I eyed her up and down. She was wearing a light pink nightie. "I'm not looking at the blanket, sweetness. Come here."

"Hold that thought. I'm going to go get my robe. I'm cold."

Before she could turn around to leave, I grabbed her wrist and sat her on my lap. "Don't worry, baby." Sliding my fingers into her panties, I rasped, "I'll have you burning up very soon."

Under all the hurt, the insults, and the things we could never take back, I still felt our profound love in this house.

I hadn't been in our bedroom for months, and once I stepped into the space we used to share, a shiny frame caught my attention from the corner of the room. Suddenly, I was walking toward the pictures I hadn't seen in who knows how long.

Did she just hang these?

Reaching for the frame, I took out the photos to hold them in my hand. It was the pictures we had taken in the photobooth at the end of the summer carnival all those years ago. We were sixteen and looked so fucking young. Her eyes sparkled against the sun coming in through the balcony behind me, only revealing her contagious smile and petite features as her hair flowed around her stunning face.

I remembered that night as if it were yesterday.

"Fuck, Kinley," I breathed out to myself. "Where did we go wrong?"

"I ask myself that every day, Christian."

I spun around, and our eyes connected. She was standing by the door, looking at me with uncertainty and sadness.

"If that were true, we wouldn't be getting a divorce."

"What? Now you think I don't love you? You couldn't be more wrong. You're the only family I have. Did you ever think about that? Do you ever think about how hard this is on me? Do you even care what I feel?"

"Of course I do."

"You're not the only one who's hurting, Christian."

"Well, you're the only one who's hurting us, Kinley."

"You want a baby. A family. And you deserve that. It's not fair that I can't give you one."

"You don't know that. It was years ago, and if you'd let my partner take a look at yo—"

"Christian, stop! Just stop!"

"Just fucking tell me how do I stop loving you?!"

—Kinley—

"I don't know, Christian! Because I don't know how to stop loving you either! I'm just so tired of not being able to say the right things to you. I'm exhausted having to walk on egg shells when we're together or else we'll fight. I ask myself every day what happened to us. You're my best friend—"

"I'm not Jax, Kinley, so let's get that straight."

"Oh my God! Are we back to this now? Jax isn't even here. He's in Miami. It's football season."

Jax had been the quarterback for Miami for the last twelve years. He was the all-star, the G.O.A.T. (greatest of all time) Getting drafted right out of college, he quickly became an overnight sensation with the world. Titled one of the most eligible bachelors by Forbes. He was an eternal bachelor, but we were still close. He'd been in my life since I was twelve-years-old, and Christian and he were still constantly butting heads for my attention.

You'd think they would have found middle ground after all these years.

They hadn't.

Although, it was better than it was when we were younger.

"We're not in high school anymore. Why do you worry yourself over nonsense?" I questioned, shaking my head. "You see his life. He has a different girl in his bed every night."

"I don't give a fuck who he has in his bed, Kinley. As long as it's not you."

"We've never even kissed! I am not having this conversation with you. It's pointless and stupid. You're just trying to find something to argue about."

"At least it has you talking to me."

"What would you like me to say? Anything I say to you turns into another fight, and I can't do it anymore. I'm over it!"

"It's so easy for you, huh? Forgetting about me, about us."

"I didn't say that!"

"You didn't have to! Don't worry, I'm packing up my shit. I'll be out of your life soon enough. You'll have the house all to yourself, exactly like you want."

"What?" I jerked back. "I don't even want this house! You're the one who insisted I keep it."

"I built this house for you, Kinley. It was never mine."

"No! You built this house for the family that we don't have. The one I can't—"

"Maybe you can have Jax move in since he's always here to pick up the pieces for you."

"Fuck you!"

He didn't hesitate, ripping our photobooth pictures in his hands.

"Noooooo…"

He tossed them on the floor in between us, and they scattered to the ground.

"I can't believe you just did that. Those are the first pictures we ever took together, Christian. How could you do that?"

He got right in my face, backing me up against the wall. "The same way you could just rip apart our marriage and then throw it away like it meant nothing."

Tears slid down the sides of my face, and he took one last look at me, spewing, "You wanted this. Remember that. You have no one to blame but yourself, sweetness."

I winced. It was the first time he'd used my term of endearment in such a hurtful way. My chest rose and fell, feeling like I was going to crumble to the floor at any second.

"Get out," I hissed, not wanting to see his face anymore.

"With pleasure." He spun around and left.

I jolted when I heard the front door slam before my feet moved on their own as if I was being pulled by a string. Falling to my knees, I grabbed all the pieces of our pictures from the photo booth that night.

I couldn't believe he'd tore apart our past.

But I was tearing apart our future.

The irony was not lost on me.

Holding the torn images in my hands, I was shaking as I tried to put them back together on the carpet. Except now, they weren't flawless and beautiful. The one that caught my attention the most was the photo where we were kissing. It had one huge tear down the middle of our faces.

Symbolizing how broken we truly were.

Piece by piece.

Bit by bit.

We were figments of who we used to be.

Throwing me right back to that night.

When he once again stitched my heart back together, not caring I was the one who was broken.

7

Kinley

Then

It was the annual back-to-school carnival in Fort Worth, and everyone from our small town was there to celebrate the end of summer. Usually, I avoided this fair like the plague, but Christian was insistent on us going and wasn't taking no for an answer. Since that night on the lake two months ago, we'd spent almost every day together when I wasn't with Jax.

I could immediately tell that Christian didn't like our friendship, not that I could blame him. We were best friends, and with all the rumors about us, I knew he had concerns but hadn't mentioned them yet. I was aware it was coming, though.

Christian and I were getting closer, and the more time I'd spent with Jax, the harsher his tone would become when he'd call me to hang out. The second I said I was with Jax, it was like night and day with his voice. He was biting his tongue, biding his time to bring it up ,and I'd be lying if I said I wasn't doing the same when it came down to asking him what we were doing and where this was going.

This was the first time I had these deep, intense feelings for a guy. Don't get me wrong, I loved Jax, but it wasn't like that between us. It was like a sister loved a brother, and the feeling was mutual. But you wouldn't think that with the way Christian and Jax treated one another.

Jax was as protective over me as Christian was. He'd already warned me about Christian, saying he was going to hurt me. Christian had the worst reputation with girls, and everyone knew it.

He was a huge player, and Jax was simply being a good friend, wanting me to steer clear of him. As much as I was worried that he would hurt me, I couldn't stay away from him. There was something about the way Christian looked at me, talked to me, made me feel that I couldn't ignore or push away.

He made me happy, triggering butterflies in my stomach every time we were together. I never wanted our time to come to an end. It was getting harder to hide my real feelings about him, and a huge part of me knew he was aware of the effect he was having on me.

Once I stepped out of Christian's truck at the fair, he waited for me by the hitch of his truck, extending his hand when I got close to him. I cocked my head to the side, raising an eyebrow. He was going to hold my hand in public, and since we always hung out alone, I was a little caught off guard by his gesture. This only confused me further as to where our relationship was going. The more time we spent together, the more I realized how much of a romantic he truly was.

"Let's go show off my girl, huh?" He grinned while I grabbed his hand.

I tried to keep my amused expression to myself as he tugged me toward him. We walked hand-in-hand into the carnival, strolling past all the rides until we were by the water. The fair was next to Eagle Mountain Marina, and he led us down to the docks.

Christian loved the boats. He was always talking about them, saying how much he wanted to own a yacht one day. When we reached the end of the boat slip, he stepped over the railing onto a gorgeous yacht.

"Whoa. I'm not down for breaking and entering."

He grinned again. "Don't you trust me?"

"Not if we get arrested for trespassing."

He laughed, nodding to the front of the boat. It was only then that I noticed there was a blanket spread out on the bow. He winked, pulling me onto the yacht.

"Wow," was all I could manage to say as I slowly turned in a circle, taking in my surroundings.

The sun had just set, and every star shined bright above the water. I took in the blanket and picnic basket that was perfectly placed in the center of the bow.

"Is this another one of your moves? Do you bring all your girls here? I can see why you get laid as much as you do." I chuckled to no avail, taking in his stern expression. "What?"

"Sweetness, let's get one thing straight, alright?" He placed his finger under my chin to get me to look up at him, and I did, anxiously waiting for what he was going to say.

"Anytime we do things together, it's the first time for me too."

I shyly smiled, his words warming my heart. Making me feel like shit for what I'd said before.

"If there's anything important you need to know about me, it's that I don't do anything I don't want to. But with you… I don't know how to explain it, Kinley. I was drawn to you from the first day you walked into my science class in sixth grade."

"What?" I jerked back. "You remember that?"

He smiled. "The girl with the turquoise backpack."

My eyes widened. "Turquoise is my favorite color."

"It's mine too."

"I didn't know you even knew who I was back then."

"Of course I knew. I was going to ask you to be my lab partner, but your best friend beat me to it."

"Oh."

"Oh? Is that all you can say?"

"Depends. Are you going to say something mean about Jax?" I blurted, unable to hold back.

He cocked an eyebrow. "So you've noticed that I don't care for him?"

"I mean, anytime I say I'm with him, your tone immediately turns sour." I shrugged. "Do you not like him?"

"I'll answer that question after you tell me what he thinks about us hanging out."

I swallowed hard.

"I think you have your own answer built in your question, Kins."

"We're best friends."

"So I've heard."

"He's just trying to protect me. You don't have the best reputation,

Christian."

"Jax needs to mind his own fucking business before I do it for him."

"Whoa." I raised my hands. "Where did that come from?" I lowered my eyebrows, confused by the turn of events. Instinctively, I peered down at the makeshift picnic he had made for us…

For me.

"I don't want to fight. Especially after you planned this beautiful picnic. I still don't know if we're going to get arrested, but you know, it's the thought that counts."

He laughed, throwing his head back, and I took the opportunity to ease his mind.

"You have nothing to worry about when it comes to Jax. I promise. But if you wanted to get to know me back in sixth grade, why wait till now?"

"You're always with Jax."

"So?"

"I don't like to share."

"Then why now?"

"Honestly… I don't fucking know. I saw you at the bonfire party, and you looked upset walking into the woods by yourself. I followed you before I even realized what I was doing. It's the effect you have on me. I lose all sense of control when it comes to you."

I smiled, and my chest seized. He'd often express the sweetest things. Still, I couldn't just open my mouth and be sincere with him, tell him what I felt, because every last insecurity that was buried deep within my bones would consume me, bordering on the point of pain.

The truth was I was falling for him. I was only sixteen but felt much older. Mature beyond my years. It had always been that way for me, having to grow up fast and mostly alone. You don't realize how much of your childhood affects the person you become, the person you are. How memories shape your life, your feelings, and most importantly your *love*.

"Do you mean that?" I asked, my heart beating fast.

"Here's another thing you need to know about me, Kinley. I don't say anything I don't mean. Since we started hanging out, I find myself doing all sorts of shit I've never done before, and I don't want it to end."

"You don't?"

"Do you?"

I shook my head.

"Words, sweetness. I need to hear you say it."

I took a deep breath, admitting, "I like being with you too, Christian. Although I can't say I noticed you in science class in sixth grade. I was a mess back then. I didn't notice a lot of things. It's why Jax is my best friend. He's the first person to ever want to get to know me, and I learned a lot about myself through our friendship."

"What's that?"

"I have a hard time letting people in, and when push comes to shove, I do the pushing and shoving. I guess it's how I survived my mother. You know?"

"I know." He was weighing his words. I could tell by the expression on his face.

"Just ask me, Christian."

"Alright. Well, what about me? You want to push me away too?"

"Yes … no… I don't know. I don't want to get hurt, and I know you definitely break hearts, but at the same time, I like being around you. These last two months have been fun, and I like you. A lot."

He smiled wide. "I like you a lot too."

Hearing him say those six words meant everything to me. I could feel my guard coming down more and more with him, and for someone who had suffered so much abuse as I had, it was a hard pill to swallow.

"How about I promise you I won't hurt you. If you promise me that you and Jax won't have sleepovers anymore. Deal?"

"You've heard about that?"

"Amongst other things."

"I can assure you that most are made-up lies. We've never kissed, we've never even held hands. Sure, we've had sleepovers, but he stays on his side of the bed, and I do the same. We don't cuddle, if that's what you're imagining. It's not like that between us. I don't feel for Jax what I feel for you when we're together. The love I have for him is just brotherly."

My heart dropped when he jerked back, and the expression on his face quickly turned somber, then he bit out…

"You love him?"

8

CHRISTIAN

I eyed her skeptically.

"You know there's a difference between loving someone and being in love with them, right? I love Jax, but I'm not in love with him, Christian."

It'd been three months since Kinley turned my world upside down and two months since we'd started hanging out.

I held her hand.

I kissed her lips.

I listened to everything that came out of her mouth as if she was telling me the world's biggest secrets.

I hadn't tried to cop a feel or get in her panties. I didn't so much as try to get her to make out with me. Being around her was enough. It was all I wanted. To be with someone, to really be with them on a level other than physical, was something I'd never experienced before. Something I never had, and I didn't want it.

The bullshit.

The emotions.

The ups and downs.

Yet there I was, officially pussy-whipped with absolutely no pussy and sporting the worst case of blue balls known to fucking man. I couldn't remember the last time I'd fucked my fist as much as I had in the last three months. Especially in the last two.

After our first talk in the woods, I'd hung out with a couple of girls, trying to forget about Kinley to no avail. I couldn't stop thinking about her, and anytime a girl attempted to kiss me, I instantly turned my face. Feeling like I was cheating on Kinley which didn't make any sense.

At that point, we'd had one conversation, but it felt like the deepest connection I'd ever had with anyone in all my life. I didn't understand any of it. The need to be around this girl was throwing me off-kilter. I thought about her constantly—the next time I would see her, talk to her, hold her…

The list was endless.

Our connection was easy, we didn't have to work at it. It wasn't a burden or a struggle to be with her like it sometimes was with other chicks. I used to get bored the minute the sex stopped, moving on to the next.

Not with Kinley, though. I wanted more. Our dynamic flowed seamlessly, our conversations, our chemistry, our *friendship*. Another thing that was new to me was being friends with a girl I was hanging out with. I never cared to get to know them. They were a means to an end.

It was simple.

Now I was in a dynamic I couldn't get enough of. One of the things I adored the most about her was the subtle looks she would give me when she didn't think I was looking.

She came into my life like a breath of fresh air, and I breathed her in like a man who was suddenly on death row. Unable to fight against her pull. Every time I was with her I was lost in us. I never expected to fall for her. I wasn't even looking for anyone, but there she was, this girl with such a force, such a drive. It was so fucking powerful that I never stood a chance.

Every time I told myself that today was going to be the time when I'd make my move, and we'd get past this PG shit, I couldn't bring myself to do it. She wasn't just another chick I could nail.

It wasn't about getting laid.

At least not with her.

Julian thought it was hilarious, laughing his ass off at the guy I'd become in the span of three months. Saying if I was like this now, he couldn't imagine what I'd turn into the longer we were together.

"Did you hear what I said, Christian?" she questioned, bringing me back to the present. When she'd just told me she loved another guy.

Fucking Jax.

"I heard you."

"Do you believe me?"

"You haven't given me a reason not to. I don't want to talk about Jax anymore."

"Good." She smiled, and it lit up her entire face. "I'm starving."

For the next hour, we ate dinner on the bow and talked about nothing in particular.

I watched the way her lips moved.

The way her hair blew in the wind, framing her face.

The way she laughed with her whole body, feeling it deep in my bones.

I especially watched the way she looked at me as I swept her hair away from her face. She didn't say a word, but her eyes spoke for her. The way she affected my mind and heart was terrifying, but it was so real.

So consuming.

She felt it too. That much I knew.

Breaking our strong connection that held both of us captive, I cleared my throat and stood up, bringing her right along with me. Something came over my senses, and I reached for my phone in my pocket to hit my playlist. Once I found the song I wanted, I set it down on the ground next to our makeshift picnic, which I'd made just for her.

With the music, the boat rocking softly, and the bright moon shining above our heads, I spun her into my arms before holding her close to my chest. Taking one of her hands, I placed it on my shoulder then intertwined the other with mine, placing it near my heart.

Her face conveyed so many emotions in a matter of seconds, and I paid attention to each and every one. She placed the side of her face on my chest, and I knew what she was trying to do, but it didn't matter because I already felt everything she was trying to hide.

"Tell me something you've never told anyone," she uttered out of nowhere.

I thought about it for a second. "I want to be a doctor."

"What?" She gazed up at me. "Really?"

"Mmm-hmm."

"Wow. You're just full of surprises, huh?"

I peered deep into her eyes. "Sweetness, you have no idea."

—Kinley—

After we cleaned up the boat which I learned was actually his parents', Christian grabbed my hand and led us back to the fair where it felt as though all our classmates were in attendance. Girls were looking at us, more like glaring everywhere we went. I was at the fair with Christian Troy, and it was a big deal in and of itself.

There we were, holding hands throughout the carnival, and he didn't do this. He wasn't this guy who was winning stuffed animals and kissing my lips every chance he had.

It was as much of a shock to me as it was to our classmates, the open affection he was showing me. He wasn't trying to hide the fact that we were hanging out.

When my eyes shifted to the photo booth by the trees, Christian didn't hesitate to take me over there.

I smiled, knowing he was doing this for me.

"Come here," he ordered, sitting me on his lap once the curtain was closed and no one could see us. We were both facing the camera in front of us.

"You feel good on top of me, sweetness."

My heart sped up. This was the first time we were this close, and I felt his dick through his jeans on my ass. I mean we'd kissed, but that was it. Which was another thing that was confusing to me. Christian didn't just kiss. He was a home run kind of guy and didn't wait around to have sex with chicks.

They threw themselves at him. He didn't have to try, but with me, he never pushed for anything other than kissing. As if just spending time with me was enough for him.

"I thought you didn't like taking pictures?" I asked, trying to calm my racing heart.

"I don't," he whispered in my ear from behind me. "I'm doing this for you."

I smiled wide, my stomach fluttering.

We took five pictures in different positions. The first was with us facing the camera. His arms were around my waist, and his face was nuzzled in my neck. I could feel his breath on my skin, igniting tingles to stir down my spine.

The next one he started tickling me, both of us laughing like fools as the camera clicked for another photo. The third picture was a funny one, where we were both sticking out our tongues. The fourth photo caught me by surprise, as Christian spun me around so that we were now facing each other.

I gasped when I realized I was straddling his waist, making him grin. Pulling back my hair, he kissed my lips, and the next two images were just of us kissing.

He rasped against my lips, "I'm going to like taking pictures with you."

Everything was perfect.

He was perfect.

"Come on." He stood us up. "Let's go on the Ferris wheel. It's my favorite ride. You get to see the whole town from the sky, and there isn't anything like it."

My emotions went from excited to anxious in a matter of seconds. I thought I could do this for him, but as soon as it was our turn to go on next, I began to internally freak out. Feeling like I was going to have a panic attack at any moment.

"Mom, please get up. Please, Mom. I need you to get up. Don't do this to me."

"Sweetness." Christian interrupted my memory. "What's wrong?"

I frantically shook my head. "I don't want to go on there."

"What?" He smiled. "Are you afraid of heights?"

The anxiety was tearing through every inch of my body. "No. Please. I don't want to go on there."

"Hey…" he coaxed, pulling me toward him. "You're shaking. What's going on?"

"I just don't want to go on there." I yanked my body away, and all I could do was run away.

Between making our first appearance together at the carnival, everything he shared, and now having to go on this ride. It was too fucking much.

I ran.

From my memories.

My feelings.

Him.

He quickly caught up to me, gripping onto my waist to spin me around to face him. "Kinley, talk to me. What's wrong?"

It was like word vomit, there was no stopping what I said next. "What are we doing?"

"What do you mean? We were going on the Ferris wheel."

"No, I mean what are we doing together?"

"Is that what this is about?"

"Yes. No. Maybe?" I shook my head. "I don't know."

"I think you do."

"We've been spending a lot of time together, and now you bring me here where our entire school is in attendance and everyone is looking at us."

"So let them stare. Who cares?"

"I do! I'm falling in love with you."

His eyes widened. "You're what?"

"Oh fuck. I can't believe I just said that. I didn't mean it."

I wasn't sure which was worse, his expression from before or the one he was giving me right then.

He frowned. "You didn't mean it?"

"No. I mean yes. I mean … I don't know."

"Kins, you're talking in circles, and it's hard to keep up."

"I know. I'm sorry. It's just this place, all these people, you, and now the Ferris wheel… I'm just overwhelmed."

"Over a ride?"

"It's not just a ride to me."

"What does that mean?"

"I can't—"

He grabbed my hand and led us over to a secluded area where there was no one around. Only us. Still holding onto my hand, he pulled me to the ground.

"Sweetness, talk to me. What's going on?"

I could see the Ferris wheel from where we were sitting, and all I could envision was the last time I was on one. There was no use hiding it from him. I'd already made a fool of myself.

"It was my tenth birthday, and my mom brought me to a fair that was in Columbus. I was so excited. She never acknowledged my birthday. I've never even had a birthday cake or been sang a song. I fucking hate my birthday. She found a way to ruin each one."

"Oh, baby…"

I might have been with Christian, but my mind was back to that night with her.

"All I wanted was to go on the Ferris wheel, and we waited for hours in line until it was finally our turn. My mom was drunk, she was always fucking drunk. Kids from school were there, and they saw the mess that she was. By the time we got on the ride, she was so wasted that she passed out, and I couldn't get her up. I tried the entire time we were on it, but there was no getting her to open her eyes." I paused, trying to shake away the look on the parents' faces when they saw her, knowing they felt bad for me.

I hated that more than anything. Their sympathy was another knife to my heart. I just wanted to enjoy my birthday. One celebration she didn't ruin. One memory I could look back on with her and feel like she was there for me. Even if it was just this one time, I had something.

Anything.

"They had to call the ambulance to come get her and pump her stomach. I spent the rest of my birthday in the ER waiting room, crying that she'd ruined yet another day for me. When I went back to school everyone was talking about it. I couldn't get away from it. Child services were called, and they showed up at our house again. It was awful. Everything with her was always so fucking awful."

Tears rimmed my eyes, and I was beyond exhausted from crying over her. Christian's gaze told me everything I didn't want to see.

"Please don't feel bad for me. Your pity is the last thing I want. You had this awesome day planned, and now I'm ruining it with my bullshit. Ugh! I'm sorry I'm so broken."

He didn't say one word. He simply grabbed my hand again and lifted me up with him. My heart was beating a mile a minute as he walked us back to the ride, nodding to the attendant to let us by. He'd recognized we were just in line and let us through.

Christian found the first empty seat, and I sat with him before he pulled down the bar. It was one of those seats where you couldn't see anything but our heads, and our bodies were covered by the steel metal in front of us.

The longer he didn't say anything, the more nervous I became.

Was he mad? Upset? Did I ruin this too?

Question after question assaulted my mind until the ride started, and around we went. Once we were up top in the air, Christian turned to me. Sweeping a piece of my hair behind my ear, he gazed deep into my eyes. I could tell he was lost in his own thoughts, and I never wanted to know what he was thinking more than I did at that moment.

I opened my mouth to say something, but nothing came out. I didn't have to wait long until he kissed my lips, trying to calm me down. His mouth felt different this time. It was soft, tender, caring. I didn't know how long we kissed. All I knew was that my reckless thoughts were fading into the background, and I was consumed in the way he was able to bring me peace.

He pecked my lips one last time before he asked against my lips, "Do you trust me?"

I nodded, unable to form words.

His other hand went in between my legs, asking again, "Still trust me?"

I nodded again.

"Words, Kinley. I need to hear you say it."

"Yes," I breathed out, hanging on by a thread.

I was wearing a dress, and all he did was place his fingers on top of my silk panties. I swallowed hard when I felt him begin rubbing me there. I trembled, and my mouth became dry as I closed my eyes.

"Eyes stay on me, sweetness. I'm going to replace the bad and make you feel so fucking good."

I opened them, and his fingers moved slowly at first. With each elevated breath that escaped from my lips, he moved them faster and more precisely, working me into a frenzy of lust and emotions.

"You're so fucking beautiful," he groaned. "Let me take care of you."

"Christian," I rasped, feeling his demanding hand until all I could feel was this urgent rush of release.

I'd never felt anything like it before. It was magical and had me seeing stars. He kissed my lips, stifling my moans into his mouth as I came fast and hard. I would never forget the words that came out of his mouth next. They would stay with me forever.

It was the first time he professed, "I'm falling in love with you too, Kinley. I'll always replace your bad memories with my love for you."

9

Kinley

Now

"I can't believe you flew in for me, Jax."

He was sitting at my kitchen island while I made him some coffee.

"Of course I flew in for you. You were bawling your eyes out on the phone last night. Where else would I be?"

He wasn't exaggerating. It'd been two days since I'd last saw Christian, and I was a mess. Unable to forget that he'd ripped apart the pictures from a night I held so dearly in my heart.

Shaking my head, I replied, "I don't know how we got here. It's like we've become these two different people I don't recognize anymore, and all I want is for it to end."

"You sign the papers in what? Three days?"

"We're not officially divorced until we go before the judge, and our lawyers can't schedule that until we sign the papers. It's not about our divorce, though, Jax. It's who we've become in these last few years. You've been there since the very beginning of our relationship. You've seen our love. He used to make me smile and laugh. Everything about us used to be so easy. We just worked well together. I don't understand where things took a turn for us."

I averted my eyes.

"What?"

"Nothing."

"Oh, come on, don't give me that. Tell me."

"I don't want to bring up the past. It's pointless."

"I want to know what you're thinking. Please tell me."

Jax deeply sighed. "Listen, I don't know the first thing about how to make a relationship work, let alone a marriage. I could be completely off base here, but one of my teammates recently got a divorce from his wife too."

"And?"

"Kinley, don't make me say it."

"Jax…"

"Fine, but just remember you made me say it."

"Jesus, what?"

"They couldn't have a baby."

I grimaced.

"See? What did I tell you? This is why I didn't want to mention it."

I had to know. "How long did they try for?"

"Years, like you guys. Except she did all the fertility treatments, and he said it made their marriage worse. She was in the worst moods, and they had scheduled sex, blaming each other every month the test came back negative. Kinley, they spent hundreds of thousands of dollars trying to conceive and, in the end, all it did was ruin their marriage."

"So what are you trying to say? It's the same for us?"

"I'm not saying shit. You're talking to a guy who's never even had a girlfriend. I'm the last person you need to be asking advice from."

"I think he blames me. Actually, I know he does."

I didn't have to express the words. Jax knew what I was referring to.

"Kinley, you didn't know what was going to happen that night."

"How could I not? You did. Christian did. I didn't listen to either of you, and look what happened."

He shrugged. "We all make mistakes."

"I should have listened. If I had, we wouldn't be getting a divorce right now."

"You don't know that."

"You just said that your teammate—"

"I know what I said, but what the fuck do I know? I don't go past the first date."

"He wants a family, Jax, and I can't give him one."

"Once again, you don't know that. Your husband is a pussy doctor. Just let him check you already. You worrying and blaming yourself isn't going to help your situation. Put your mind at ease. At least for the future."

"I don't need a doctor to tell me what I know. Besides, I already—"

"That was over ten years ago, Kinley. Medicine has come a long way since then."

"It's not going to change anything."

"That's bullshit, and you know it. You guys still love each other, anyone could see that."

"Sometimes love isn't enough."

"I don't fucking like him, I've never liked him, but at one point, he made you really happy, and it was all that mattered to me. I hate seeing you like this, and it's only going to get worse once you sign those fucking papers."

"I'm fully aware you don't like him. I had to practically beg you to come to our wedding, remember?"

"It was during the season. You know football always comes first."

"Speaking of that. What are you doing here? You're still in season."

"I'm catching the redeye back." He winked. "My girl needed me, so I'm here. Football may come first in my life, but you come a close second."

"I'll remember that the next time I'm begging you to do something you don't want to."

"You're getting a divorce. There's no reason to beg me for anything anymore."

I sighed, changing the subject. "So who's the flavor of the week?"

"It's football season. You know I don't fuck during the season."

"You're still doing that?"

"Makes me play better."

"Right … all that pent-up aggression, Mr. All-Star. Are you going to win the Super Bowl yet again?"

"I wouldn't be Jax Colton if I didn't."

"You don't sound very excited about that. You're a free agent in two years, and I say you come play for Dallas."

"We're back to this?"

"Yes! You can play for your state. Can you imagine the press? They'd have a field day, and people would eat that shit up. Your fanbase would grow by the millions."

"I don't need any more people kissing my ass, Kinley."

"I know."

"And I could do less with the press these days. Most of the time, I want to break their fucking cameras."

"Yeah, they're getting worse. I can't believe how they hound you. You're all over the gossip shows and magazines."

"Fuck that gossip bullshit. Do you have any idea how many lawsuits I have with them? The shit they make up on a daily basis for views and sales. I practically pay their bills."

"Well, maybe if you wouldn't sleep around with every model within a five-mile radius they wouldn't have anything to report on you."

He grinned. "More like every one-mile radius, but who's counting?"

"Obviously you."

He laughed. "For someone who's getting a divorce, you're very fucking chipper."

"My best friend is in town. Of course, I'm chipper. I haven't seen you in months. I miss you, and for completely selfish reasons I'd love for you to move back to Dallas."

"I'll think about it."

"Good." I smiled. "How're your parents?"

"My mom still asks for money every chance she gets, and my dad sells bullshit stories that never happened to the press. Other than that, they're peachy-fucking-keen."

"I'm sorry you have to deal with that."

"I'm sorry you have to deal with Christian. Is there anything I can do? You want me to kick his ass? 'Cause you know I'd love to. I've been wanting to fuck him up since your seventeenth birthday when he sucker punched me."

"Oh God, don't remind me." I turned around, grabbing his coffee from my espresso machine. I didn't want to think about that now. I had enough to deal with. "You still take it black, two sugars?"

"Yeah."

I reached for the canister that held the sugar, but it was empty. Grabbing the stool from the pantry, I placed it in front of the cabinet where the extra sugar was and stepped on it. The floor was still damp from when I'd mopped it that morning, and it slid right out from under me.

"Shit!" I shrieked, but Jax was quick on his feet, catching me in his arms before my ass hit the ground.

I opened my mouth to thank him but was cut short. The garage door flew open and both of our eyes snapped toward the disruption. My heart dropped, sinking to the bottom of my stomach. I locked eyes with the man I least expected to see.

His seething glare shifted from me to Jax, who was still holding me close to his chest. From an outsider looking in, it appeared as if he'd caught us in an intimate moment. However, it couldn't have been further from the truth.

"I'm going to fucking kill you!" was the first thing I heard Christian say since he'd tore apart our photo booth pictures.

—Christian—

They moved away from each other while I lunged toward Jax at the same time.

"It's not what you think!"

Before the last word left her mouth, my fist was connecting with his jaw. Kinley loudly gasped as his head whooshed back, taking half of his body with him. He stumbled, trying to catch his footing while meeting my intense rage.

His hands quickly fisted at his sides.

"What the fuck is he doing here?!" I snarled through a clenched jaw. "This is still my house."

"You need to calm down!" Kinley demanded.

"Calm down?! You want me to calm down when I just walked in on my wife in the arms of her best friend?"

I went for Jax again, but she stepped out in front of me.

"No!"

"Kinley, get the hell out of my way!"

"Yeah, Kinley! Get the fuck out of his way. I would love to finally lay him out!"

"Jax!" She snapped around. "Stop it! You're not helping."

"He's just trying to take advantage of you. How can you not see that?"

"He is not! I was getting him sugar, and the stool slipped. He caught me before I fell to the ground. You should be thanking him. I could have been in the ER if it wasn't for Jax."

"It'll be a cold day in hell before I ever thank him for anything."

"Christian, please…"

"Kinley, he's trying to break us up."

"No, asshole," he spewed. "You did that all on your own."

"Oh my God. Stop it! Please!" Her panicked stare went from him to me and back to him. "I've been getting in between the two of you for the last twenty years, and I'm over it. You're grown-ass men, so stop acting like children."

"Fuck him!" I roared, my blood seething. "Stay away from my wife, and get the fuck out of my house!"

"She won't be your wife in a few days."

"You son of a bitch. That's what you want, isn't it? It's what you've always wanted—her to yourself and me out of the picture."

"Do you hear yourself, Christian? That couldn't be further from the truth, and you know it! He's been nothing but a good friend to me all these years. Why can't you see that?"

"Maybe it's time she knows what a real man can do."

"Jax!" she shouted, looking back at him. "Where the fuck did that come from? You're just making things worse!"

I once again lunged at him, and she gripped onto my arm, holding me steady.

"He's not a child, Kinley. Let him come at me like a man," Jax baited, and if she wasn't standing in between us, I'd wipe the floor with his ass.

"What are you even doing here?" I asked, demanding to know.

"What the fuck do you think I'm here for? I'm here for her." He sternly nodded to Kinley. "She was bawling her eyes out over your ass last night."

"She was?" I was taken aback.

After what I did with our first pictures, I was surprised she was anything other than pissed off. It was one of the reasons I was there in the first place. I wanted to apologize.

I fucked up, and it seemed like lately it was the only thing I could accomplish when it came to her.

Jax read my mind, spewing, “Yeah. How many times can you treat her like shit and then apologize for it, huh? You’re lucky I don’t knock your ass out for all the times you’ve made her cry in the last year alone.”

“Fuck you, Jax. You have no business getting involved in our marriage. You fuck anything with tits and an ass, so don’t try me with your martyr bullshit. But what you can do”—I pointed to the door—“is get the fuck out of my house.”

“It’s not your house anymore—it’s hers.”

I didn’t just fall back from his statement. I stumbled.

I must have been quite a sight since Kinley coaxed, “Christian…”

Our gazes locked for a few seconds, and I could physically see and feel her internal struggle about what he’d just stated. She opened her mouth to say something, and I held in a breath.

Tell him he’s wrong, sweetness.

She didn’t.

Silence.

Scoffing out in anger, I slowly nodded and backed away. There was nothing left for me here, not even her.

All I could do was remind her, “We haven’t signed the papers yet. This is still my house. But I can see I’m no longer welcome here, so I’ll make it easy for you, Kinley. I’ll leave. I’d hate for you to make the wrong decision of choosing him over me.”

She winced, only fueling my fire for what I was going to maliciously add…

“We all know what happened the last time you didn’t choose me.”

10

CHRISTIAN

Then

A year came and went in the blink of an eye, taking all our new firsts with it. I spent as much time as I could with Kinley. She was at my house all the time, and my family loved her. I'd never forget the expression on my little sister's face when I introduced her as my girlfriend a few weeks after the carnival.

"Wow," Autumn expressed with wide eyes. "Christian has never come home with a girlfriend before. You must be super special."

Kinley laughed. "And you must be Autumn."

"I'm the little sister." Autumn nodded. "My birthday was just last week. I'm ten now."

"I know." Kinley smiled. "I went with Christian to pick out your present."

Autumn beamed. "You did? How did you know I loved Littlest Pet Shops?"

"Doesn't everybody? They're my favorite too."

"Really? Maybe we could play with mine."

"I'd love to."

"Christian," Mom chimed in, bringing our attention over to her. She

was standing beside my dad, looking as captivated as I was by my girl. "She's absolutely beautiful."

"Thank you, Mrs. Troy."

"Oh please, call me Emma."

"Yes, and you can call me Steven," Dad extended his hand.

For the rest of the evening, we hung out as a family, and I could tell Kinley appreciated being around them. I thought it was the first time she had been around a dynamic like ours.

Later that night, she proved my theory.

I was sitting on the couch with her head in my lap, playing with her hair while we watched a movie.

She turned her face to look up at me. "I had a great time tonight. Thanks for introducing me to them."

I smiled. "Sweetness, you don't have to thank me for introducing you to my family. They've been dying to meet you."

"Really?"

"Of course. They all wanted to meet the girl who now owns my balls."

She slapped me on the chest. "Christian!"

"What?" I grinned, teasing, "You know I'm fucking with you. Only I own my balls, baby. But you…" I winked at her. "You can definitely own my cock."

Her mouth dropped open. "What about your heart?"

"Well, that too."

"Christian," Autumn announced, bringing me back to the present. "I think you should get her the turquoise birthday cake since that's her favorite color."

I nodded. "I think you're right."

"Jesus fuck," Julian exclaimed. "Where did your balls go, man? Did you just hand them over to her?"

Autumn giggled. "My brother loves Kinley. She's his soulmate. Do you think you have a soulmate, Julian?"

"Nah, I'm not made like that, kid."

"Maybe you already know her"—she shrugged—"and you just don't know it yet."

"I don't know many girls."

"Bullshit." I chuckled. "You know every girl with tits and an ass from here to Dallas."

"I've banged every girl from here to Dallas. Doesn't mean I know them."

Autumn scratched her head. "What does bang mean?"

I hit him in the chest, only looking at her. "Nothing you'll ever do."

"I don't think I'd like to bang," she remarked. "It doesn't sound very nice."

Julian laughed from deep within his chest, and I resisted the urge to hit him again. I swear he'd forget my little sister was only eleven, she was still a kid, and I wanted to keep her that way for as long as I could.

Autumn was beautiful, even as a baby. I knew there would come a time when little shits would be knocking on our door to take her out on a date, and I'd have to threaten their lives if they didn't keep their dick in their pants.

"Christian, do you bang? Does Kinley?"

I glared at Julian, who was suppressing another laugh.

"Why don't we let your brother pay for his turquoise birthday cake."

"It's not mine, you dick. It's for Kinley's seventeenth birthday."

"So you've said." He nodded to Autumn before getting down on one knee for her to jump on his back. "We'll meet you outside."

"Don't let her out of your sight."

"He's giving me a piggyback ride! I think that counts, right?"

"It counts, kid."

I watched them leave before grabbing a box of condoms. We hadn't had sex yet. I could tell Kinley was getting impatient, waiting for me to make a move soon, so I figured it was better to be prepared just in case. I didn't know why I was holding back, when we'd done everything else. I just wanted to make it special for her.

Fuck, I really did turn into a pussy.

Shaking my head, I paid for my stuff and then dropped Autumn and Julian off at our house. Julian was watching Autumn for the rest of the day while my parents were at work.

I was surprising Kinley with balloons, gifts, and a cake for her birthday. Knowing it was the first time she'd experience anything like this.

By the time I made it to her house, it was after three, and I knocked on her door.

Completely caught off guard…

When Jax opened it.

—Kinley—

"Christian!" My eyes lit up, taking in his huge display of birthday balloons. "Geez, did you leave any in the store?"

"What are you doing here?" he asked, nodding to Jax.

Shit.

"It's my best friend's birthday, Christian. Where else would I be than with my girl?"

Christian stepped up to him, and Jax didn't hesitate, standing taller. Not backing down.

"She's not your girl, asshole."

"Whoa!" I wedged myself in between them. This was me in the last year, having to constantly play referee when they were around one another. "It's my birthday! You guys don't get to pee on me today."

Their stares never wavered from each other.

"Come in," I said to Christian, opening the door wider for him to walk through and making sure Jax was still behind me.

It wasn't like Jax couldn't carry his own with Christian. I didn't want it to get to the point where fists were flying.

As soon as we all walked into the kitchen, Christian's eyes shot to the half-eaten turquoise cake Jax had brought me that morning with the blown-out candles lying beside it.

"What?" I asked, taking in his sudden harsh expression.

His glare cut to Jax. "Did you know she's never had this?" Before his gaze snapped to me. "Because if he did know, then this wasn't just a coincidence. He's trying to show me up."

"Christian, he's my best friend."

"I'm supposed to be your best friend."

I winced. "Please don't be this way."

"If you knew she's never celebrated her birthday, then why now?" he accused Jax. "Huh? You've been *best friends* for the last five years. Why the fuck now? Unless you're trying to prove a point to me?"

Jax snidely smiled. "I don't have to prove shit. I know where I stand in her life. Can you say the same, *boyfriend?*"

"Enough!" I intervened. "I'm tired of having to choose sides with both of you. This is ridiculous. We can all celebrate together."

"Why now?!" Christian roared.

"I didn't like celebrating my birthday before this year!" I declared for Jax. "You've changed that in me. Your whole family has. I wanted to celebrate my birthday for the first time with both of you. Is that a good enough answer for you?"

"I can't believe you don't see what he's actually doing, Kinley. It's fucking obvious."

"I'm not doing shit," Jax argued. "Instead of asking me if I knew, which I did, I've been trying to get her to celebrate her birthday since I met her. But what you should be asking yourself is why you're so fucking insecure about it?"

It happened before I even saw it coming. I swear I blinked, and Christian's fist was slamming into Jax's jaw.

"No!"

Jax flew back, catching himself on the kitchen island.

With wide eyes, my hands flew to my face. This wasn't going to end well, that much I knew. I lunged toward Jax to help him, but Christian grabbed my arm, stopping me.

"What the fuck? You're going to him?"

I abruptly turned around. "You're the one who hit him!"

"No shit, and I'll do it again."

With his hand on his jaw, Jax moved it around, scowling, "I'd like to see you try."

"I just did!"

"You fucking sucker-punched me, you bitch!"

"Please stop!" I begged. My heart was pounding profusely. Two of the most important people in my life hated each other with the same love I had for both of them.

This was the last thing I wanted to happen on a normal day, let alone my birthday.

"Get the fuck out!" Jax ordered. "You're not wanted here!"

My stare flew to Jax. "What?! I want him here!"

"You want me or him, Kinley?"

"Christian!" I exclaimed, staring at him now. "That's not fair!"

"You want to know what's not fair, Kinley? That he's purposely doing this to make us fight, and you can't see it!"

"No, he's not," I affirmed. "You don't know him like I do. You're just being unfair."

"Fine," Christian bit out. "I'll fucking leave." His vicious expression tore back to Jax, glaring him down with a look I'd never seen before from him. "But don't for one second think we're done here. I'm only leaving because I love her, and if I don't, I'll lose her…"

His next words rendered me speechless and broke my heart at the same time.

"*To you.* Exactly the way you want."

11

CHRISTIAN

Now

I took a swig off the bottle of Jack as I made my way into the bathroom of the bar. The fiery liquid burned with delight, and all I wanted to do was forget. Tomorrow we'd sign our divorce papers, and despite knowing we still needed to go before the judge to make it official, it didn't matter.

Our marriage was over. The rest was simply logistics.

Then what were the last twenty years for?

I fixed the broken girl only for her to shatter me in the end.

I'd tried kidding myself into believing I wished the last fucking twenty years didn't happen, but that was a lie because there I was, thinking about only her.

My wife.

The only woman I'd ever loved.

I wanted to imagine that I didn't see her face in front of me, the same face I'd woken up to every morning and fell asleep with every night. She'd lay in the crook of my arm while I played with her hair until she passed out.

It was the best part of my day. Having her in my arms was what I looked forward to the most. I'd watch her sleep, taking in her beauty.

However, if I would have known the last time I made love to her would have been the last I'd feel her mouth against mine, her heart beating in sync with mine, her body beneath me with my cock inside of her…

I would have taken more time to hear her moan, make her come, ruining her for any other man in her future. The mere thought ignited an intense fury I'd never felt before. A dark torment settled over my mind. It coursed through my veins, pumping through my blood as I took a long hard look in the mirror, not recognizing the man staring back at me anymore.

Who was he without Kinley?

We'd been together for so long, all I knew was how to love her.

Protect her.

Have her standing by my side.

For better or for worse didn't matter anymore. Our vows were just words now with no meaning.

No value.

No morals.

The void in my heart spread like wildfire through my bones, deep into the core of my being.

I couldn't stop the memories of her messy, unruly hair partially covering her face when I'd wake up every morning to her pouty, pursed lips which were usually swollen from my relentless and insatiable assault on her mouth the night before.

Her face flushed.

Her naked bare skin.

It was all a reminder of how many times I'd made love to her.

The scent of sex used to always hang heavy in our room. I could never get enough of her, and there was a time when she couldn't get enough of me either. Only fueling my memories of how perfect we used to be together.

Both of us held captive by our love for one another.

I was such a lucky bastard. Having Kinley was all that mattered.

How do I stop loving her? How do I make the fucking pain go away? How do I live without her?

My heart ached thinking about all the questions that constantly hounded me. The fire inside of me would only ever belong to her. My core seized up thinking about the passion we once had for each other.

The longer I stared at myself in the mirror, the more the bathroom started to cave in on me, and I was finding it hard to fucking breathe.

The walls tightened all around me, stirring this piercing pain that felt as if I'd carry it with me the rest of my life. It was now a part of me, like she'd always be.

Along with the guilt of what I could have done differently.

The memories of where we went wrong.

The demons that we couldn't conquer and the new ones that we were taking on.

It didn't matter how hard we tried, or how much therapy we went to, nothing changed the outcome of us not being able to have a baby.

She was right. I did want a family more than anything in this world, but I didn't want it more than I wanted her. She didn't believe me, and I knew she was still carrying the trauma from her mother.

The thought of that woman sent my blood fucking boiling.

Searing.

Scorching my skin from the inside out.

I was certain about one thing and one thing alone—when I signed those papers tomorrow, I'd be taking her love with me.

I stood there battling the desire to go home to her, fully aware it wasn't my home anymore. She made that perfectly clear the last time I saw her with Jax of all fucking people. Every emotion hit me in the face, back to back. Taunting me. Playing me like a goddamn fiddle. Making me feel like I was nothing more than a piece of shit.

And her soon-to-be ex-husband.

The truth slammed on top of me, my adrenaline triggering me to jump into action. I could feel the sweat pooling at my temple as I walked out of the bathroom. Chugging down the already half-empty liquor bottle in my grasp.

"Dr. Troy," a familiar voice called out.

I turned to find a young brunette striding toward me with lust in her eyes. Like she'd just landed a prize. And just like that, it was gone. I could breathe.

Was this what I needed to officially move on?

She laughed. "You don't remember me, do you? Well, I guess that makes sense considering you're usually looking at my pussy."

Did I just hear her right, or was I completely hammered?

I was used to women coming on to me, but this one was brazen with her words and her actions. I didn't look like your average OB-GYN. I was covered in tattoos, sleeves down each of my arms. As a kid, I used to love tattoos, and the second I turned eighteen, I spent it at a tattoo parlor, getting inked for the first time.

Kinley was by my side when I got our anniversary tatted on my chest in roman numerals. There were several tattoos on my body that symbolized my wife.

What the fuck do I do with them now?

The woman leaned in to me, throwing her arms around my neck. "You look so lonely all by yourself, Dr. Troy. But you're in luck! I'm such great company."

This was the first time in two decades that another woman was touching me so intimately, and all I could think about was Kinley.

Even in my drunken state, the woman throwing herself at me looked young.

"How old are you?"

"Old enough," she baited, looking up at me through her long, dark lashes. "I could help you forget about your ex-wife."

It didn't surprise me she knew about our divorce—we were the talk of our small town.

I grabbed her arms from around my neck. "She's still my wife."

"My name's—"

"I don't care what your name is."

She ignored my response, stating, "Let's go back to my sorority house."

"Fuck me," I breathed out, but she misinterpreted my reply.

"I'd love to."

"No." I shook my head. "I need to go—"

"Yessss! Let's dance!"

I blinked through my haze, and we were suddenly on the dance floor, her ass grinding on my dick while she backed me into a wall. Everyone's faces were blending, and I could barely see a foot in front of me. Before I knew it, I was back in the bathroom, except this time I was standing in one of the stalls.

The sound of my zipper tore me out of whatever alcohol-infused blackout I was in. Looking down at the ground, I jerked back and zipped up my slacks.

"What the fuck?"

"What the fuck is right!" the woman seethed. "Why won't you hook up with me? I've been trying all night, and all you keep doing is blowing me off! What's the matter with you? Your cock wasn't even hard when I was dancing on you!"

I didn't have time for this bullshit, yearning for my wife. I left her there, on her knees, yelling obscenities, and tuned her out.

By the time I realized where I was, I was somewhat sober and walking into what used to be my house. Through my drunken state, I walked inside, and my feet moved on autopilot until I was opening the door to our bedroom, catching Kinley by surprise.

She gasped, spinning around to face me with her arms over her bare breasts. "Jesus, Christian! You just scared the shit out of me!"

For the first time in I didn't know how long, I fucking smiled, gripping the door handle. Cocking my head to the side, I took in her gorgeous wet body from the shower. She looked better than I remembered.

And trust me, I fucked my fist to the sight of those tits so many goddamn times.

"Christian, what are you doing here?"

I nodded to her breasts. "I've seen them, baby. I've sucked on them, have come on them, and I've fucked them. You remember, don't you? Because I have no problem reminding you again, sweetness."

Her eyes widened, taking in my dominant stance. "You're drunk."

"And you're fucking beautiful."

She shook off my compliment. "Did you drive here?" Grabbing her silk robe off the bed, she threw it on, and I groaned, wanting to keep her naked and wet.

Kinley looked out at the driveway through the balcony slider I'd made love to her against time after time.

"Oh my God! You did drive here! What were you thinking?"

"I wasn't."

She jumped when she realized I was standing behind her, and I turned her to face me.

Except, she swept my hands away. "I'm going to make you some coffee. I can't believe you drove here like this. If you get pulled over, you could lose everything."

"I already lost everything. Thanks to you."

"That's not fair."

"How do you turn it off, Kinley? How do you just stop loving me? I need you to tell me. You owe me that much."

She sidestepped me, but right when she took a step, I grabbed her arm and tugged her into my chest.

Instantly, her face paled as she placed her hands on my shoulders. "You smell like whiskey and women's perfume." The expression on her face turned lethal when she wiped something off my neck, showing me red lipstick on her fingers. "Oh. My. God. Were you fucking someone before you came here, Christian?"

"Kins." I snidely grinned. "You lost the right to ask me about who I'm fucking when you decided you didn't want me fucking you anymore."

She gasped, jerking back. "I can't believe you came here after being with another woman! You fucking asshole! How dare you?!" She went to slap me across the face, but I caught her wrist in the air.

Using her momentum, I spun her around and pressed the front of her body against the balcony slider door. Her back was now against my chest.

"You remember the first time I fucked you against this window?"

Her breathing hitched.

"You were wet from the shower, just like you are right now, and I couldn't help myself. I never could with you. You know that, right? The effect you've always had on me?"

Her breathing became erratic, and it started to fog up the glass on the side of her face. "Did you say that to the whore you were with tonight? I know what you were like before me, so I can only imagine how slutty she was."

"If you must know," I snidely chuckled. "She was a sorority girl."

"You shameless bastard!"

Thrusting my hard cock into her ass, she loudly gasped again.

"Are you jealous, sweetness?"

"You fucking asshole! Is that why you came here, Christian? To throw your whore in my face?"

"Hmmm…" I groaned into the side of her neck, breathing her in. "Naked and wet was always my favorite Kinley."

"Fuck you, Christian."

I connivingly smiled. "I'd much rather fuck you, baby. I wasn't with another woman tonight. I couldn't stop thinking about your perfect tits, your luscious ass, and that tight fucking pussy I love so much."

"How noble of you," she gritted through a clenched jaw. "I'm not stupid. You have her lipstick all over your neck and smell like cheap perfume."

"Nothing happened."

"I don't believe you."

"I don't lie to you, Kinley. You know that like you know my name."

"It doesn't matter. After tomorrow you can fuck anything that walks."

"You mean like your best friend does?" I scoffed out, having to remind her about the truth of who I was. "I changed for you, sweetness. I became the man you needed me to be. After I met you, I gave up who I was. *For you.* How can you think I could just fuck someone else after all that? I don't even know that man anymore. I don't know who I am without you, Kinley Troy."

She shut her eyes, feeling the sincerity of my words burning into her skin. "I never asked you to do that."

"You didn't have to. You want to know why?"

"Why are you doing this to me?"

I didn't hesitate in telling her another fact, "Because *this* ... is all I have left of you."

"Fine, Christian. You win, okay? I'm the bad guy. I'm the fuck up! This is all my fault! Is that what you need to hear?"

"You haven't listened to one thing I've said, so I'll make it easy for you. I fucking love you! Do you hear me, Kinley?" I didn't hesitate in adding…

"There is no me without you."

—Kinley—

I did the only thing I could in a moment when I needed him to let me go. Even though I didn't mean it, I spewed, "You want to know what, Christian?"

"What, baby?"

"You being with your sorority girl tonight just made me realize I don't love you anymore, okay? There! You got what you came for. Now leave!"

He growled as my heart pounded in my ears. I couldn't believe I'd just said that. The lie tasted like vinegar on my tongue, like acid on my heart, like a knife to my soul.

I never expected what happened next. He abruptly turned me around to look at him, slamming my back against the slider. I grimaced from his rough assault.

But at the same time, I welcomed it.

Repeating, "I don't love yo—"

Except, this time he cut me off.

Crashing his mouth onto mine.

12

Kinley

His hands dug into my hair.

It was intense.

Forceful.

Demanding.

As his tongue devoured my mouth.

My memories didn't compare to this and what was unexpectedly happening between us. I should have stopped him. I should have pushed him away and kicked him out of my house. I should have done anything other than grip onto the front of his shirt, yanking it open. Buttons flew in every direction, cascading down on the tile floor.

Wanting him closer like he wasn't already close enough, I ached to mold us into one person. Kissing him back as if my life depended on it. I moaned into his mouth, losing myself to his skilled tongue and lips. It had been forever since we were like this.

The passion.

The emotions.

I couldn't remember the last time we consumed one another quite like this.

"Fuck…" he groaned into my mouth. "Do you have any idea how

much I miss this? How much I miss you?"

With a strong force taking over me, I suddenly shoved him away. Not wanting to hear another sad story. Our lives were already filled with them.

All the mistakes and regrets.

All the hurt and devastation.

All the I'm sorry's and I love you's.

The ups and downs.

They were endless.

Timeless.

Destroying us both in the process.

He reached for me, and as soon as I felt his arms wrap around my waist, I pushed him as hard as I could. His back hit the slider with a hard thud, and I didn't falter.

I went for him.

"Why can't you just let me go?!" I hit him, all over his face and body. Anywhere I could.

He blocked each advance, only triggering me to hit him harder and with more determination. Beating out every ounce of frustration and love I still had for him.

All the years of pent-up anger.

All the times we went to bed angry.

All the things we'd said to hurt each other, when in reality … it killed us to say them.

"Kinley, calm the fuck down!" he ordered, trying to grip onto my wrists.

"No!" I yelled, striking and shoving him the closer he tried to come toward me. "Can't you see this is killing me! This is my fault we're in this place, Christian! I'm the one who can't give you babies!" Hot tears shot out of my eyes. "I'm fucking broken! I've always been broken, and I'm so tired of you trying to put me back together! It's not fair to you! I've never been right for you!"

Thinking back on the night that drastically changed the course of our lives, I cried out, "I should have listened to you! Why didn't I just listen to you?! What's wrong with me?!"

In my defeated state, I wasn't strong enough to hold him back any longer. In an instant, he spun me around, gripped onto my wrists, and held them above my head, pinning me against the glass slider.

"Do you have any idea how many nights I've stayed awake thinking about that very question?! Why couldn't you have just listened to me?! Month after month of negative tests! There it was! That same fucking question! I have spent years thinking about that night! I could have lost you too!" he roared, his body shaking. "Can't you see? I don't fucking care! I'm blind for you! I'm mad for you! I fucking ache for you! Why can't you see that all I want is you, Kinley?! Why is that so fucking hard for you to realize?"

Those profound words were all it took for me to lose my shit.

I slammed my mouth onto his, biting down on his bottom lip until I tasted blood.

He immediately jerked back, holding my wrists with one hand while the other yanked my hair by the nook of my neck. I panted, frantically trying to gather my bearings from his tight, possessive hold. Both our bodies trembled with undeniable fire.

Every part of our resolve was hammering all around us.

Breaking.

Shutting down.

Making it hard to see, let alone stand.

I didn't know if it was our truths and lies, or the fact that I was in his arms that had me feeling fucking alive.

Thriving.

Living.

With my husband's mouth against mine.

Weakly, I thrashed around, ignoring the pain in my head and the throbbing in my heart. The damage I'd caused for both of us as we were gasping for air.

Frustrated.

Overwhelmed.

Frenzied with each other.

Closing my eyes, I tried to steady my breathing, my thoughts, my fucking heart. It was broken. Torn into a million pieces.

He loosened his grip, slowly brushing his lips against mine and causing me to open my eyes. I saw all our memories fly through his gaze, one right after the other.

The first time we talked.

The first time he kissed me.

Touched me.

Made me his.

I was born to be his…

When his heated, tormented stare became too much for me to take, I turned my face, but he gripped onto my chin and forced me to look at him again.

"You don't get to hide from me, Mrs. Troy."

I grimaced, those two words killing me slowly.

We stared at one another for what felt like hours, both of us lost in our own darkness.

In our own demons.

In our past.

In the things we couldn't change, but frantically wanted to, and in the things we could change but didn't know how.

Our future.

Our regrets.

Our love.

It was right there, ripping us apart. Piece by piece, bit by bit, we were bleeding out for each other. He licked away the blood from his lips, and I silently wished I was doing it for him. My eyes followed the movement of his tongue, stirring a rush of adrenaline to surge through my veins.

"I love you! I fucking love you!" I shouted, and he let me go, but only to once again slam his mouth onto mine.

He growled, parting his lips. His hands went to the sash of my silk robe, opening it. Making me whimper, he fell to his knees in between my legs and licked from my opening to my clit.

"Fuck…" I moaned, falling apart at the seams.

When he placed my thigh onto his shoulder, my hands instantly fisted his hair, tugging it to the point of agony.

I wanted him to feel what I was feeling.

The pleasure and the pain.

Rocking my hips forward, I felt his tongue push into my opening while he peered up at me with a predatory regard. His eyes were dark and dilated. His hand kneaded my breast as he sucked my clit into his mouth, immediately moving his head in a side-to-side, back-and-forth motion.

"Ah!" I hissed.

My chest heaved, and my mouth parted with the precise manipulation of his assault on my core. His mouth was literally eating me alive. I watched with hooded eyes as he slid two fingers into my soaking wet pussy, causing my legs to shake and my body to shudder.

Which only made him finger fuck me harder, lick me faster, wanting me to come in his mouth.

He licked me one last time, and then the son of bitch stopped, and I whined in refusal.

I was almost there.

So close.

"Please…" I shamelessly begged, wanting this for myself.

Christian was the only man who'd ever touched me, kissed me, made me his. I didn't know anything but him. He knew my body better than I did, learning and memorizing it for hours on end.

"You think another man is going to make you beg for what's always been mine?"

I panted profusely, my chest rising and falling on bated breath.

"Tell me. Say the words, Kinley."

I didn't have to be ordered twice. "I'm yours, Christian. I'll always be yours."

He growled and returned to lapping at my heat, making me go crazy with need. Within seconds I was coming apart, fast and hard. Shaking the entire time. I rode out my orgasm against his mouth before he released my clit with a pop.

Not bothering to wipe away my come from his face, he attacked my mouth instead with his hand planted firmly at the back of my neck, keeping me locked in place. Close to him, exactly where I wanted to be.

I tasted myself all over his lips and tongue, unable to get enough of what only he could bring out of me. Gripping onto my ass, he lifted me up to straddle his waist and shoved my back against the slider again.

The glass shook, echoing in the room.

"You remember the first time I fucked you against this glass?" He grabbed a fistful of my hair. "You were mine then. Exactly like you are now. No matter what, Kinley Troy, I'm embedded in your blood."

Our mouths crashed together as I undid his belt. Working the button and zipper of his slacks, unable to get them open fast enough. I pulled out his hard cock and aggressively stroked it in an up and down motion.

He wasn't the only one who knew me inside and out. I knew him too, and Christian loved it rough.

His hand went to my throat and the other on my hip, gripping hard and applying ample pressure to both. He wanted to mark my body, remind me who I belonged to…

And God help me, I wanted him to.

"Please, Christian … fuck me like you used to."

It was all he needed to hear.

In one swift, hard thrust, he was balls deep inside of me.

"Fuck," he loudly groaned against my parted mouth as I hissed into his, crying out but not saying a word.

We hadn't made love in who knew how long, and I'd forgotten how big he was. Digging his fingers into my ass, he rolled my hips to have me fuck him harder and faster. There was nothing sweet about what we were doing to each other.

We were angry fucking, and I never wanted it to stop.

He mercilessly pounded into me. "This what you want, Kinley? For me to fuck you like this?" The slapping sound of our skin-on-skin contact echoed in our bedroom. "You want me to fuck you like you're mine?"

"Yes..."

"That's it, baby … squeeze my cock with your tight little pussy that I can never get enough of. Just like that. I want to feel you come on my cock."

With every thrust inside me, I felt the mass of his body movement inching me a little higher on the glass. I savored the feel of his dick splitting me open. I knew I wouldn't be able to walk in the morning without feeling him there.

My pussy throbbed against his shaft while my G-spot pulsated along the head of his cock. Over and over again.

"I'm going to come," I rasped.

Our ravenous bodies and rage had taken over. My back hit the slider again and again. We were both spiraling out of control in a frenzy from the feel of our mouths and bodies colliding. Coming together as one. He felt it as much as I did. It lingered in our chaos.

Each thrust.

Every moan.

Each push and pull.

Brought back memories neither one of us could ever forget.

He fucked me harder and with more determination, his heart beating fast against mine. Kissing me passionately with everything left inside of him.

"Ah! I'm going to come…" I shut my eyes.

"Eyes stay on me, sweetness. Let me take care of you."

His words brought me back to another place and time when his dick was inside of me for the first time. Caging me in with his arms against my head, he looked deep into my eyes, and I showed him everything he needed to see.

I panted, and my body shuddered the closer I got to release.

"You're tight, little pussy was made for me, baby. How many times have you thought about this? About my cock deep inside of you? I showed you how to come, Kinley. I showed you everything you love." He slammed into me, using my hips as leverage and making me keep up with his vigorous pace.

"What do you think, baby? Should I just stop and leave you like this? Maybe then you'll know what you're doing to me. Maybe then you'll feel me dying for you. Maybe then you'll finally admit you don't want this fucking divorce."

He never once let up on his ruthless thrusts. One by one, I began to come down his cock.

"I'm coming… I'm coming… I'm coming…" I breathlessly panted, fighting back the tears from how true his statement was.

"Yeah, Kinley … just like that. Squeeze my fucking cock like my good girl." Another growl escaped from deep within his chest, as I milked his cock to come right along with my orgasm.

He roughly thrust in a few more times before our bodies went lax, breathing heavily on one another. Our thoughts running marathons, mimicking our fuck session that happened out of pure anger and desperation to feel some sort of connection to each other.

I reveled in the feeling of him still inside of me, not wanting this to end.

It didn't.

Christian carried me over to the bed, and for the next several hours we made love as if we were those two crazy kids who only needed one another.

He made love to me until there wasn't any love you left to express.

Until there wasn't an inch of my skin he hadn't kissed or caressed.

Until there were no pants, no moans, no growls or groans.

He made love to me until there was nothing left inside of me but his come.

I fell asleep in his arms while he played with my hair like he'd done for so many years.

Except when I woke up, he was gone.

And all that was left…

Was to sign our divorce papers that afternoon.

13

CHRISTIAN

Then

A week had gone by since Kinley's birthday, and I'd barely seen or talked to her. This was our first big fight, and I didn't know what to say or do to make it better.

I wasn't going to back down on how I felt about Jax and his intentions with us. He didn't want us together, that much I was sure of.

"You're like a love-sick puppy, Christian. Where the fuck did your balls go?"

"Fuck you, man."

Julian laughed. "Just apologize and go down on her. Works like a charm."

"Right, because you would know."

"You're right, I wouldn't, but if I was in the dog house, I'd use the only weapon I have. My skills to make her see God."

"How do you see God?" Autumn walked into my bedroom. "I want to see God. Can you make me see God?"

"Autumn, the day you see God is the day I go to jail."

She rolled her eyes at me. "I'm not going to be your little sister forever, Christian."

"I hate to break it to you, but you'll always be my little sister."

She rolled her eyes again. "Julian, can you tell him that one day I'm going to have a boyfriend, and he's going to love me something fierce?"

Julian narrowed his eyes at her. "I'm going to go with your brother on this one, kid. No little shit is going to make you see God on our watch."

"What does God have to do with having a boyfriend? We're not even religious."

I laughed, I couldn't help it. The shit that came out of her mouth was hilarious.

"Are you guys still fighting?" Autumn asked, sitting on my bed.

"Can you not tell? Look at your brother, he looks like my worst nightmare."

Autumn narrowed her eyes at me. "I think you should go to her house, tell her how sorry you are, and then remind her of why she loves you."

"You think it's that simple?"

"Christian, love is easy. It's you who's making it hard."

"Bro, you just got schooled by an eleven-year-old."

"I'm almost twelve, Julian, if you haven't noticed."

"Twelve." He smiled, appeasing her. "Such a big girl."

"Only three more years and I can have a boyfriend."

"Says who?" I countered, eyeing her.

"Our parents."

"Over my dead body."

"Christian! I'm allowed to be in love too!"

"At fifteen, you're not going to be in love, Autumn."

"Why not? You were."

I jerked back from her response, realizing she was right.

For the rest of the day, I thought about Kinley until I suddenly found myself on her doorstep.

Taking my little sister's advice.

—Kinley—

I opened the door. "Christian," I breathlessly stated, at a loss for to me.

My heart fluttered, my stomach dropped, and my mouth parted the moment he greeted, “Hey, sweetness.”

I hid back a smile, unaware of how to proceed with him. Blurting, “What are you doing here?” instead.

He flinched from the sharp tone of my voice, not trying to hide his emotions, unlike me. Which had always been a consistent trait with Christian. He never tried hiding from me. Always showing me his true colors.

I didn’t know what to say. We’d barely spoken since my birthday, and when we did it was short and awkward. Neither one of us knew how to proceed. This was a first for both of us, and it was obvious with how we were acting with each other.

I didn’t want to lose him, but I didn’t want to lose Jax either, and it was unfair he expected me to choose.

I was allowed to have friends outside of him, and he needed to understand that if things were going to continue between us.

“I can’t stop thinking about you,” he expressed out of nowhere, warming my heart. “I’m sorry about your birthday, Kinley. That wasn’t supposed to happen.”

“I know.” I nodded, leaning against the doorframe. “I’m sorry too. I hate fighting with you. Especially over Jax. It’s so silly, Christian.”

“The last thing I want is to talk about Jax right now.”

“Then why are you here?” I asked in a detached tone.

“Come on.” He cocked his head to the side with a sly grin. “Who do you think you’re talking to?”

“What do you want me to say?”

“That you forgive me.”

I swallowed hard, taking in every last word that fell from his lips. By the expression on his face, he was being sincere.

“I love you, Kinley, and I don’t want to lose you. Especially to fucking Jax.”

“How many times do I have to tell you it’s not like that between us?”

“Then prove it to me.”

“How?”

He smiled, stepping into my house before closing the door behind him to lean against it. “By letting me have another one of your firsts.”

I arched an eyebrow, smirking. “What are you saying, Christian?”

Leaning forward, he whispered in my ear, "I want to make love to my girl."

"Whoa, you go from zero to a hundred like no one I've ever met before."

"Let me take care of you, sweetness."

I thought about it for a second. "What happens after?"

He grinned. "I make you come again."

"Christian." I blushed. "You know what I mean."

With another honest expression, he vowed, "I'll love you forever."

"What about Jax?"

"What about him?"

"He's still going to be a big part of my life."

"As long as I have a bigger part in it, then we won't have a problem."

"Of course. I want to love you forever too. I'm yours," I stated with sincerity.

"Not yet, but you will be soon." With that, he gripped onto my ass and pulled me against his body. Wrapping my legs around his waist, he walked us back to my bedroom.

He knew we were alone. My aunt was at work. She was always at work.

With each step he made toward my room, I felt the butterflies bubbling in my stomach. I wasn't nervous, more like anxious for what was to come.

"I missed you," was all I could say as he laid me down on my bed before he hovered over my small frame, caging me in with his arms around my face.

"I missed you too, baby."

I was only wearing a flimsy sundress, and it was easy to throw over my head after he kissed me. Once I was naked, he eyed me with a predatory regard that had my thighs clenching. He did this to me every time I was bare for him, as if he was taking me in for the first time.

I loved it.

Nobody made me feel what Christian could. At seventeen-years-old, I was already aware no one else ever would.

I could sense he was hesitating probably on my behalf, knowing this was the first time for me. I wanted to feel him in every possible manner. I had for months now, but he never tried more than just us messing around.

He respected me, and coming from a guy like him, it meant everything.

Recognizing his uncertainty, I made it easy for him. Tugging his lips back to mine, I coaxed, "Touch me, Christian."

"Where?" he said into my mouth.

"Anywhere you want."

He smiled as he slipped his tongue past my parting lips. Working it in ways that had my legs spreading and wrapping around his waist. My arms quickly followed, doing the same around his neck.

No space or distance between us.

He kissed me gently, adoringly, fervently.

Christian pulled back a little, resting his forehead on mine to look deep into my eyes. There was a hunger in his stare that I'd become familiar with. Although he wasn't even touching me, I felt him all over.

I craved his touch.

His taste.

The feel of him on top of me and in between my legs.

All his adoration.

His love.

Devotion.

Every laugh.

Smile.

Everything and anything.

I just wanted *him.*

Reaching for the front of his shirt, I helped him pull it over his head to toss on the floor next to my dress. My fingers pressed against the pulse of his neck, wanting to feel it beating only for me. I stayed there for a few seconds, slowly skimming them down to his heart and then his taut abs until I reached for his belt.

The warmth and softness of his skin made my sex clench and my stomach flutter. The butterflies he always stirred never got old. It was one of my favorite emotions he evoked.

The feelings he ignited inside of me were what fairy tales were made of. I never thought I'd find a love like his.

Like ours.

14

Kinley

I thanked my lucky stars he came into my life when he did, making me believe I was worth being loved. I grew up on my own, with my mother constantly calling me a burden, annoying, saying she wished she'd never had me.

When you'd heard it enough, you started to believe it. I spent years telling myself I wasn't an accident or a mistake, I had a purpose, and maybe it was to save her from her own madness.

I tried for years and never could, yet still … I wished I had.

Her voice messages on our answering machine were getting more persistent, and little by little she was beginning to stir that desire to have her in my life again.

She said she was sober, clean, and taking her medication.

The little girl in me wanted to believe her, but I'd heard it all before, too many times to count. Her lies always sounded like truths. No matter how many she told me, I couldn't tell the difference.

"Hey…" Christian stressed. "Where did you go?"

"I'm sorry." I shook my head, covering my face. "I'm ruining this."

"Babe." He pulled my hands away. "What's going on?"

"Nothing."

"Kinley, don't hide from me."

I sighed. "I don't know. I was just thinking about how lucky I am to have you in my life, and it brought on these memories of my mother telling me I was worthless." My eyes widened. "Here you are, wanting to make love to me, and I'm thinking about my mom. Jesus… I'm so fucked up. I'm sorry, Christian."

"What did I tell you the first time I put my hands on you?"

"That you'd always replace my bad memories with your love for me."

He smiled. "Always, sweetness. I'll protect you from everything, especially your mother."

I didn't need to hear anything else. This was perfect.

He was perfect.

Reaching for his belt, I gasped when he unexpectedly gripped my hand and stopped me.

"Are you sure?"

Before I could assure him, tell him what I felt so deeply in my heart, how much he meant to me, how much I wanted to be his and only his, how much I wanted him to own me.

Mind.

Body.

Soul.

He hoarsely murmured against my lips, "Sweetness, I've never been with a virgin before."

"Really?"

"Yeah. I never wanted to take that from a girl."

I softly chuckled. "You're saying all the right things."

"I don't want to hurt you."

"You won't." Again, I repeated the words he needed to hear from me, "I trust you."

He let go of my hand, and I unclasped his belt. Next was his zipper before he kicked off his jeans and boxers. I reached for his dick, but he moved my hand out of the way.

"This isn't about me. It's about you, Kinley."

His gaze set me on fire, and my heart kicked into overdrive. I loved the way he was looking at me. He had my heart in his hands, to do with as he pleased, and I'd remember this moment for eternity.

I knew right then and there I would never be able to go without him. He was my always and forever.

Licking his lips, he leaned in to kiss me. The second his tongue touched mine, my back pushed further into the mattress. My legs spread wider for him while he placed all his weight on his arms that were cradling my face.

"You're so fucking beautiful, Kinley. How did I get so lucky to have another one of your firsts?" He started to place gentle kisses down my cleavage and toward my nipple, sucking one into his mouth as his hand caressed the other.

Chills ran up and down my spine as my back arched off the bed, wanting more, and he happily obliged. I could feel his erection on my wet core, and he purposely moved his hips, grinding against my heat, and creating a delicious tingling that I felt all over.

I moaned, already falling apart which earned me a forceful yet tender caress of his hand against my clit. He manipulated my bundle of nerves, and within seconds my legs began to shake, and I couldn't keep my eyes open.

"Eyes on me, sweetness."

I opened them as he effortlessly made his way down my body. Once his face was in between my legs, he pushed his fingers into my opening and sucked my clit into his mouth in a back and forth motion.

My hands immediately gripped his hair, and he grunted in satisfaction. I couldn't take it anymore. The room started spinning and my breathing became erratic.

"Ah … mmm…" was all I could manage as I exploded on his tongue in a mind-blowing orgasm.

The next thing I knew he was kissing me, and I tasted myself all over his mouth. He knew my body better than I did, spending hours upon hours exploring it until he'd memorized every last curve and what I liked.

I heard a rustling of some sort and opened my eyes to see that he was opening a condom, but I stopped him.

"I'm on the pill."

He arched an eyebrow.

"I've been on it for the last two months, wanting to be prepared for this moment. I don't want anything between us, Christian. I want my first time to be skin on skin with you."

"I've never gone raw before, Kinley."

I smiled wide, feeling this surge of emotion tear through my veins.

"Then I'm taking one of your firsts too."

He slammed his mouth onto mine, giving me exactly what I craved, and placed the tip of his dick at my opening.

"I love you," he whispered in between kissing me.

"I love you too. More than anything," I murmured, not breaking our kiss and eye contact.

I moved my hips, beckoning him to keep going, yet still, he didn't move an inch, and I started to worry.

However, when I felt his hand move lower toward my clit again, I began to relax. His fingers played my over-stimulated nub, and seconds later he slowly eased his way inside me. The sensations of his fingers replaced the uncomfortable feeling of his thrusts.

I was done for.

There would be no coming back from him.

I was his.

Exactly the way I wanted.

"Are you okay?" he groaned into my mouth.

"Hmm…"

"You're so fucking tight, so fucking good. You were made for me, baby."

—Christian—

Nothing compared or even came close to the feeling of Kinley on my cock. This was more than just sex, more than just two bodies coming together, more than anything I'd ever experienced before.

This was her.

Mine.

I patiently moved in inch by inch, trying to take her as slowly as I could, wanting to cherish her the way she deserved. I hated hearing about her mother and the things that woman had put her through.

If I'd ever met her, I wouldn't be able to hold back from telling her she was a sorry ass excuse of a mother.

Shaking away the thought, I wanted to focus on the present and the feeling of Kinley wrapped around me for the first time.

"Almost there, baby." I thrust in a little more. "I love you," I reminded, wanting to give her a bit of comfort.

"Mmmm…" was all she could reply.

"There," I whispered, nuzzling her neck. "I'm inside of you, sweetness. Can you feel me?"

"Yes…"

Not stopping the friction of my fingers against her clit, I uttered, "There's my girl."

I moved my fingers faster while gradually thrusting in and out of her.

She was so fucking tight.

So fucking wet.

So fucking perfect.

My thumb brushed against her cheek, and she smiled as I kissed the tip of her nose, thrusting a little faster. I grabbed the back of her neck to keep our eyes locked.

My forehead hovered above hers as we caught our breaths, trying to find a unison rhythm. My thrusts became harder and rougher, her body responding to everything I was giving.

What I was taking…

Claiming.

Her eyes dilated in pleasure but also in pain, and I immediately lapped at her breasts, unable to stop myself from devouring her.

"Christian," she breathed out, and I swear my cock got harder.

I moved up to her face, and our mouths were parted as we both panted profusely, clinging onto every sensation of our lovemaking. I felt myself start to come apart, and she was right there with me.

"I love you," she repeated over and over, coming down my balls and on the bed, taking me right over the edge with her. I shook with my release and passionately kissed her again, wanting to savor this moment a little longer. We stayed like that for I don't know how long.

I kissed all around her face.

Her neck.

Her breasts.

Once it was time to go to the bathroom, I carried her in there with me and turned on the shower.

To take care of what was mine, now and forever.

15

CHRISTIAN

Now

I walked into our lawyer's office like a man on death row. I could still taste Kinley on my fucking tongue as I made my way into the conference room of this godforsaken building. When I didn't see her sitting there, for a moment I thought she'd come to her senses and she couldn't go through with this.

After what happened last night, it was obvious she didn't want this divorce either. She was just too fucking stubborn to admit it. However, my hopes were dashed when I saw her out on the balcony that overlooked the lake behind the building.

The second I stepped outside, I took a long, deep breath, feeling as though I couldn't breathe again. Kinley was against the railing, her shoulders were hunched over, and her body was slightly trembling. I could hear her soft cries through the breeze in the air, only further proving my point.

She was still mine.

Normally, seeing her like this would have made me feel content, knowing she was hurting like I was, but at that moment, it was the complete opposite effect. I didn't want this for her, and I felt awful she was breaking down, here of all places.

Where we'd sign our divorce papers, and it'd be the end of us.

"Christian, I know you're behind me," she declared, not turning around. "I can feel you. Do you think it will always be like that? Me being able to feel you when you're near?"

"I hope so."

She shook her head, scoffing out, "Is that why you came to the house last night? To make me feel like absolute shit right now? We made love all night and now … now we're about to sign divorce papers, and all I can think is what the fuck are we doing? Even with all the shit I went through as a child with my mother, I've never felt so lost before."

"Then come back to me, sweetness."

Her breathing hitched as soon as she felt me come up behind her shuddering frame. She didn't turn around, and she didn't move. She was frozen in the spot she stood, aware that if I touched her, she'd break down in my arms.

I closed my eyes, waiting for I didn't know what. Feeling her devastation on every inch of my body was by far the worst pain I'd ever experienced. We weren't even touching, yet I felt her all over.

Her sadness.

Her uncertainty.

Especially her love for me.

I leaned in, just inches away from her neck, and let my breath brush against her ear, causing shivers to course through her and her knees to buckle.

She wrapped her arms around her stomach in a comforting gesture. Her emotions were threatening to spill. Our vows were revealing themselves. I wanted to consume her with my presence, wanting her to feel afflicted.

Conflicted.

So she'd miss my touch.

My voice.

My love…

"We don't have to do this, baby."

"Yes, we do."

"Why, Kinley? Why are you doing this to us? Look at you. You don't want this. You can't even fucking look at me right now."

in a whirlwind of emotions. Battling with my heart to move or to stay grounded on what I wanted.

Needed.

Couldn't live without.

Her eyes followed the movement of my strong arms as they came around her body. Skimming the sides of her ribs, I placed my hands on the railing out in front of her.

Caging her against my body, my scent, my ink that was permanently covered on my skin, proudly displaying our life together. My chest piece was memories of us, and the closer I got to her, the more I could feel her turmoil burning a hole into my chest. I could sense she wanted me to put my hands on her, but I couldn't bring myself to do it. If I did, I'd never be able to let her go again.

I had no words.

All I had left was devastation.

I didn't want to touch her…

But I couldn't help myself.

Again, I never could when it came to her.

—Kinley—

The floodgates opened, and I let out everything I held in so deeply. Tears began to stream down my face, falling to the ground with my heart in his hand. As if he couldn't hold back any longer, he began to slowly caress up and down my arm. Grazing my skin with only the tips of his fingers like he was testing himself.

It was so fucking ironic because last night he touched me everywhere for hours on end.

With his hands.

His tongue.

His lips.

Yet now, it was almost like I was a piece of glass in the palm of his hand he didn't want to break.

When he slid his grasp toward my shoulder and then down my back, I didn't say one word, terrified he would stop if I did.

"I love you, Kinley Troy," he rasped in a devastated tone I'd never forget.

I sucked in a breath, feeling his mouth on the back of my shoulder, as his lips casually glided up to the side of my neck. Softly, he let his lips linger on my skin for a few seconds before he pulled away just enough to trail soft kisses up toward my face.

I couldn't take it any longer.

His words were killing me, but his touch was destroying me.

I abruptly turned around, faintly pushing him away. His eyes told me he wanted to say so much, though nothing came out.

"We can't do this anymore, Christian. Last night shouldn't have happened. It wasn't our beginning. It was our ending."

"You're so full of shit, and you know it."

I shook my head. "I'm not. Nothing has changed. I can't give you children."

"We can adopt, or we can get a surrogate. We can still be a family."

"I can't do that to you. Please … try to understand. I'm just trying to do the right thing. I can't have you resenting me more than you already do."

"That's not true."

"You know it is. I've spent the last ten years thinking about that night and what I did to us."

"Kinley, I asked you to marry me that night too."

"I know." I nodded. "But we were young and thought our love would prevail."

"It still can. All you have to do is walk out of this building with me and never look back."

I immediately saw it, his eyes glazed over, and his pupils dilated. He leaned over again, caging me in with his arms to rest his forehead on mine.

"Where's my girl, huh?" He pulled the hair away from my face, staring intently into my eyes.

That did it to me every time.

There was so much emotion behind his gaze. I knew they mirrored mine.

At this point, there was no need for words—we'd said them all.

He grabbed my face in between his hands, caressing my cheeks with his thumbs. Pulling me close to his body, he held me in his arms, and we stayed like that for I didn't know how long.

I was the first to break the silence. "Our lawyers are inside. They're waiting for us. We've already spent thousands of dollars and months to get here, Christian."

"It doesn't mean shit to me, Kinley." With trembling lips, he added, "All I want is you. I love you. I fucking love you," against my lips.

"I know." I held onto his wrists. "I love you too. But sometimes, love just isn't enough."

He pulled me into his arms again, wrapping his body around my small frame. It still made me feel so safe, protected, like nothing could ever happen to me if I was in his secure embrace. Moments later, we cried in each other's arms, mourning everything we ever had together.

Our past.

Our present.

Our love.

For the family I couldn't give him.

And the future we'd never have.

I was gasping, hyperventilating, trying to breathe, trying to move, trying to find the will to walk into that building and sign those papers.

When all of a sudden, he pecked my lips, kissing me for the last time. There was something absolutely devastating about the way his mouth claimed mine.

It was slow.

Torturous.

Each caress of his tongue, push and pull of his lips, was killing me in the process.

The sun started to fall behind the horizon of the hills. Darkness settled upon us. My mouth began quivering, physically feeling his agony and the damage I was causing him. Forever making me fucking hate myself for what we were about to do.

But I had to be strong.

For him…

He deserved that much.

My face frowned as he pecked my lips one last time. There was something about knowing this was the last time I'd feel his mouth, his touch, his breath, his skin, his scent.

Him.

That truly felt like the end of my life and everything I'd ever wanted.

"I'm so sorry, Christian. I'm so fucking sorry."

He nodded, stepping back while we looked at one another.

In the blink of an eye, his eyes turned cold, detached, violent. "You want this, then you lead the fucking way."

I grabbed my face, feeling like I was suffocating. I didn't want this. I swear I didn't want this, but what other choice did I have? I was doing this for him. After all these years, it was my turn to be his savior. I stood there, desperately trying to catch my bearings, composing myself as best as I could before placing one foot in front of the other and walking into that building.

For the next hour, I blanked out.

It felt as if I was having an out of body experience.

I was there but I wasn't.

Cognitive dissonance saved my life more times than I cared to remember. I just never imagined my defensive instincts would protect me from him. I came to when I heard him slam his pen on the conference table, realizing that my stare had been glued to the document in front of him the whole time.

His signature was now below mine.

Bright.

Bold.

Standing at attention.

It's over. Your marriage is over.

At the end of our love story, all Christian said to me was…

"I hope you're fucking happy. You got what you wanted."

With that, he turned and left me there.

Alone.

Shattered.

Once again, the broken girl he couldn't save from herself.

16

CHRISTIAN

Then

"Congratulations! We're so proud of you guys! Just one more picture!" Mom celebrated, much to my annoyance, but I played nice for her.

We had just graduated from high school, so it was the least I could do.

"Honey," Dad reasoned. "You have like three hundred pictures already."

Julian and I nodded in agreement.

"I know, but our babies are growing up."

"Oh, honey…" Dad pulled her into a tight hug.

Kinley beamed, looking at my parents adoringly. I knew she admired their marriage. She loved being around them any chance she could get.

"Mom," Autumn chimed in, standing next to fucking Jax. "If you take any more pictures, we're not going to make it to lunch, and I'm starving."

Of course, he was there with us.

The worst part was, my parents actually liked him. My mom thought he was sweet and lonely, and she basically invited him to all our family functions which I couldn't do anything about.

He made Kinley happy, and at the end of the day, that was all that mattered to me.

"Okay, okay," Mom surrendered. "Just a few more of Christian and Kinley."

I smiled and threw my arm around my girl as I tugged her toward me.

"Smile. Oh, come on, Christian, smile!"

"I am smiling," I griped, unable to take much more, my face fucking hurt from smiling so much.

"You guys look so nice! Now give her a kiss!"

I did.

"Christian!" Mom chastised. "There are children around! Don't grab her butt!"

Kinley giggled, pulling away from me.

"Great, are we done now?"

"Yes, my impatient son."

Thank fuck.

"You're going to thank me when you have these amazing photos to look back on one day. You're just like your father. You have the most beautiful smile too. You used to love pictures as a child. I don't understand what happened."

I glanced at Kinley, wanting to smile for her, but her gaze was captivated by someone behind me.

I never expected what happened next, only ruining our graduation.

"Babe, you oka—"

"Mom," Kinley announced out of nowhere, making my body snap around to the woman who was suddenly walking toward us.

All eyes flew to her mother. In my head, I'd built her up to be this monster, but the woman walking toward Kinley was pretty.

Normal.

Not what I thought she'd look like.

Her hair was pinned back, and she was wearing a nice dress with a bag hanging off her shoulder. She appeared put together.

Sober.

My gaze went back to my girl, who was standing there frozen with wide eyes and an expression I'd never seen before. I didn't know what came over me, but I stepped out in front of Kinley and placed her securely behind my back.

Her sorry excuse of a fucking mother stopped dead in her tracks.

"Christian," Kinley exclaimed, surprised by my action.

"What the hell are you doing here?" I snapped at her mom, incapable of holding back.

I'd seen Kinley bawl her eyes out too many times to give a flying fuck about this woman.

"Christian!" Mom reprimanded, grabbing my arm to yank me away from her, but I didn't move an inch.

I was rooted to the ground. After what she'd put my girl through, she had no business being here now.

"Please, excuse my son," Dad apologized for me, and I resisted the urge to tell him he didn't owe her a damn thing. "He's very protective of your daughter."

She cautiously smiled. "I'm happy to hear she has such great friends—"

"I'm her boyfriend."

"Oh, well I'm glad she has someone to protect her."

I didn't falter. "Somebody has to."

"Christian..." Mom tried to get me to move again, but she didn't need to that time.

Kinley stepped out in front of me instead.

—Kinley—

"Mom, what are you doing here?"

"It's your graduation, Kinley. I'm here for you."

Those words rang in my head over and over again. "For me?"

"Yes, sweetheart, I'm here only for you."

I didn't know what to say. I barely knew how to feel. I hadn't seen or talked to her since they took me away from her over six years ago. My heart was beating out of my chest the longer I stood there taking her in. She looked better than I'd ever seen her.

I didn't recognize the woman who was standing in front of me, yet I knew she was my mother.

"How did you know where I was?"

"I talked to your aunt. She was working today, and I didn't want you to not have family in the stands." Her eyes lit up. "I watched your entire ceremony. I'm so proud of you, honey. You graduated with honors. I always knew you'd accomplish amazing things. You were always such a smart little girl."

My eyes connected with Jax. He was standing behind her, his concern for me radiated off of him. It was almost as bad as Christian's.

"I'd love to go to lunch. Catch up. It'll be my treat. You can pick anywhere you'd like to eat."

"Your treat?" I asked, confused. She couldn't hold down a job, we were always broke.

"Yes! I have a job. I've been working at a doctor's office for the last three years in Dallas. It's where I live. I'm his receptionist."

"You live in Dallas?"

"You didn't hear my messages or read my texts?" She shook her head, pretending like it didn't hurt her to hear me say that. "You know what? It doesn't matter. We can just start fresh, Kinley Care Bear."

I winced, hearing her call me that. I used to love the Care Bears as a child. They were my favorite show to watch.

"Honey, I've missed you so much." She stepped toward me, and I didn't move, cemented to the ground beneath me.

"You look beautiful, Kinley." She reached for my hair. "Your hair has gotten so long, and your face has changed, baby."

"Yeah," Christian scoffed out. "That's what happens when you lose custody of your kid and she doesn't want anything to do with you for over six years."

"Christian!" I exclaimed, surprised he was acting like this.

I never considered how he would feel if my mom ever came back into my life. A huge part of me never thought this moment would even happen, but at the same time, I was immensely grateful it had.

I'd missed her more than anything in this world.

She was my mom.

Plain and simple.

I still worried about her. Growing up, our roles were reversed—she was the child, and I was the parent. I didn't have to defend her to Christian. He should have understood this wasn't his place to have an opinion.

It was mine.

"I can only imagine what you've heard about me," she stated, meeting his eyes. "I completely understand your apprehension, but I mean

Kinley no harm. I was such a mess back then, but I'm not like that anymore." Her gaze shifted back to me. "I'm sorry for everything I put you through. I … ummm… I'm so embarrassed. All I want is a second chance with you. Please give me the opportunity to prove to you that I can be the mom you need. The one you've always wanted. I want so badly to prove to you that I've changed. I'm not that woman anymore, I swear to you."

Despite hearing this all before, I desperately wanted to believe her.

She was my mom, and I loved her.

So I simply stated, "Okay."

But Christian snapped, "You've got to be fucking kidding me?"

All eyes shot to him again.

"This woman does not deserve—"

I interrupted him, looking at his family. "I'd like to speak to Christian alone please."

His mom leaned in and kissed my cheek before his sister hugged me from behind.

Once they were gone, I peered at my mom. "Do you know where Louie's is?"

She beamed. "Yes, the restaurant in town."

"Can you meet us there?"

"Yes, of course. I'll meet you anywhere."

"Okay." I smiled. "I just need to talk to Christian really quick. I'll meet you there soon."

"Thank you, Kinley Care Bear." She drew me into a tight hug, and I melted into her embrace.

I'd lost count of how many nights I'd wished she was around to hold me, hug me, make me feel like she loved me. She held me close to her chest, closer than I'd felt in a long time. I could feel the tears forming in my eyes.

Her warmth.

Her scent.

Her love.

It was comforting and afflicting all at once.

The second she pulled away, I felt the loss of her touch. For a split second, I was scared I'd never see her again.

As if reading my mind, she vowed, "I promise I'm not going anywhere this time."

I nodded, needing to hear that.

She turned around and left. It was only then I realized Jax was now standing next to Christian.

"Jax, can I talk to Chr—"

"Fuck no. I've known you longer than him, and I'm not leaving until you come to your senses."

"Not you too."

"What did you think I was going to be like? Why are you letting her back in so easily?"

"I'm not."

"Jax is right, Kinley."

"Wow," I breathed out. "I never thought I'd hear you say those words. What is this? Two against one?"

"Baby, you're just forgiving her like all the bullshit she put you through didn't happen."

"People make mistakes."

"How many does she have to make until you cut her off?"

"What do you think I've been doing for the past six years? Christian, you didn't have to treat her like that."

Jax intervened, "The fuck he didn't. Kinley, come on. I know you miss her, but you need to keep your guard up with her. You don't know if she's—"

"No! You don't know! You have no idea what it feels like to not have a mom."

"Actually, I do."

"Jax, your parents are still in your house. You still see them every day. You still know they're there. It's not the same."

"Jax isn't saying anything that isn't true."

"Don't give me that bullshit! You"—I pointed to him—"of all people have no idea what it's like to grow up without a mother. I've never seen her look the way she does right now. She's sober and on her meds. I can tell. She was a great mom when she was clean and taking her medication. I can't just turn my back on her."

"Why not?" Christian spewed. "She did to you."

"She's sick! It's not her fault her brain isn't wired like yours. I have to give her a chance to be in my life, and it's completely unfair that you expect me not to."

"Sweetness, I just don't want you to get hurt."

"Agreed," Jax added. "I don't want that either."

"Since when do you guys agree on anything? Since when do you guys even like each other? This is the most you've said to one another since we started dating. Why can't you guys just be happy for me?"

"It's not about being happy for you, Kinley. It's about being worried for you and what's going to happen if she hurts you again."

"Christian, you don't know that she will. Besides, it's not your choice to make. It's mine! This is none of your business."

He jerked back, offended. "None of my business? Since when is protecting you none of my business?"

"You don't have to protect me from my mother."

"She's the one I have to protect you from the most!"

I took a deep breath. "Please, I just need you to support me on this, okay? She's my mom. I love her, and if she's trying to make things right between us, then I have to give her a chance."

"How many chances does she get?"

"You don't understand. You come from two loving parents and a happy home. I never had that. This is my chance to finally have what you do. Maybe her losing me the last time is what she needed to get her life in order. She's healthy, and what matters is that she's here and sober."

"Sweetness, I don't trust her."

"Yeah, Kinley. You know how much I hate to agree with Christian again, but he's right. I don't trust her either."

I backed away from both of them. Disappointed was an understatement. They had no right. This was my choice, not theirs, and it was ridiculous they thought I'd listen to them.

I did the only thing I could do, I made myself damn clear as to what my intentions were.

"Well then, you guys can stay here and bond over not trusting her together. I'm—" I spoke with conviction…

"Leaving to have lunch with my mother, with or without either of you."

Now

I opened the door to find Autumn standing there.

"Hey, what are you doing here?"

She smiled, holding onto her pregnant belly. She was in her third trimester. "This kid thinks my uterus is a punching bag. I need to pee."

I laughed. "Come in. You know where the bathroom is."

"I'll be right back."

I watched her wobble away.

Autumn was the cutest pregnant woman, all belly. She was the same way with their first daughter, Capri. Now they were having a boy, and I'd be lying if I said I wasn't jealous that she could get pregnant so easily. Don't get me wrong, I was very happy for them. They'd spent years apart and were able to find their way back to each other. You didn't hear about love stories like that every day.

She met me in the kitchen, setting her purse down on the island. "I'm dying. This is what death feels like."

I laughed again. "That bad, huh?"

"I think it's just I was so young with Capri that it was easy. You know?"

"Yeah, it's easier to bounce back too, but you're still really young, Autumn."

"Twenty-nine is not that young, and I swear this kid is all Julian. Stubborn, demanding, doesn't ever listen to me."

"Sounds like your brother."

She lovingly smiled. "How are you holding up?"

"Is that why you're here?"

"Well, I mean, you guys do go before the judge this afternoon, right?"

"Four o'clock."

She looked down at her watch. "So that means you have six hours to change your mind."

"Autumn," I coaxed. "Not you too."

"Kinley, Christian is miserable. He's not sleeping, he's barely eating, he's drowning himself at the hospital. He leaves before dawn and doesn't get back to the ranch until midnight, sometimes later."

I wiped down the counter. "That's just Christian, Autumn. He's a workaholic."

"I know." She sighed. "He gets it from my dad. He's just trying to provide for you, though. He means well. You know how much he adores you. He always has. When I was a little girl, I used to admire you guys' relationship so much. I wanted what you had."

"And look, you ended up with his best friend."

"Yeah … who would have thought, right?"

"I did."

"What?"

I nodded.

"No way."

"I never told you this, but on your seventeenth birthday, I saw him follow you out into the woods."

She gasped. "You did?"

"Who do you think kept Christian away from you?"

"Oh my God! Why didn't you ever tell me?"

"We didn't really get close until you had Capri, and by then I didn't want to bring him up."

"I can't believe you never told me."

"Julian thinks he was all sly when it came to you, but he wasn't. I could always tell he loved you."

"Really?"

"Of course. What's not to love?"

"Well, the same goes for you and my brother, Kinley. I know you don't want this divorce. The whole family knows you don't want this divorce. You guys are just going through a rough patch."

"It's more than a rough patch."

"Marriage is a lot of work—I don't have to tell you that. Especially with a man like my brother. He's bullheaded and super aggressive, but he loves with all his heart and soul. You've been together for twenty years. That's a very long time to be with someone, and trust me, half the time I want to kill Julian. Especially now with all these hormones, and he thinks I'm the world's most beautiful pregnant woman."

"You are."

"I'm not. I'm a whale."

"Autumn, you've barely gained, what? Twenty pounds?"

"Twenty-two."

I teased, "Such a whale."

She held her belly. "I think I have to go pee again." She thought about it for a second. "Wait, no. It's gone. False alarm. What were we talking about?"

"Wow. Mommy brain is real."

"You have no idea. I forget everything. Thank God for Julian, or I'd forget to take all my vitamins."

"Awe, he makes you remember?"

She swooned. "He brings them to me in the morning with water and breakfast."

"I think that's the cutest thing I've ever heard."

"It's the least he can do! I'm carrying his soccer player of a son who thinks my uterus is a soccer ball. Plus, he wants to have sex with me, like all the time! There's barely any room for this baby and my organs."

I laughed, I couldn't help it.

"It's not funny! I don't need another thing inside of me! Everything turns into sex. He rubs my feet, his dick's inside of me. He gives me a back rub, his dick's inside of me. He thinks I'm like a fucking pinball machine that he can poke all day long."

"And you love it."

"Ugh," she dramatically exclaimed. "God help me, I do. We're going to end up with ten kids, watch."

I jerked back. "Ten?"

"Oh yeah! If it were up to Julian, we'd have at least seven. He's already talking about our next baby, when this one isn't even born yet."

"He's going to give you some time to recover, though?"

"I wish! Last night he was talking about how awesome it would be to have two kids under the age of one."

"Wow."

"Right? He's insane. And don't get me started on Capri, who isn't any help either. She's ecstatic about having a brother. Especially since she doesn't have any cous" —she caught herself— "shit, I'm so sorry. Mommy brain again."

"You don't have to apologize, Autumn. I know how excited she is to have siblings. Capri is a doll, and she's going to be an amazing big sister."

"Look at me." She shook her head. "I came here to talk about you and all I've done is talk about myself."

"I appreciate the distraction."

She sat on the stool. "How are you doing? Like for real? Don't give me the bullshit version."

I inhaled a deep breath before sitting on the stool beside her. "To be completely honest, since we signed our divorce papers two months ago, I've been a fucking mess."

"Is there anything I can do?"

"You're doing it. You've been checking in on me every week. Your mom and dad come by every other. I didn't expect to still have you all in my life."

"Kinley Troy! Of course, we're still going to be in your life. We're family. No matter what is going on with my brother, you'll always be my sister."

I smiled, needing to hear that. Other than Jax, Christian's family was all I had. I couldn't lose them too.

"It's not too late to change your mind. It's obvious you don't want this divorce. And I know—you guys have had some issues with … you know, conceiving."

"Did he tell you that?"

"No, Christian is a very private man. He wouldn't tell me that, but I'm sure he's told Julian. Why didn't you tell me?"

"Autumn, you didn't even live here until a couple of years ago when you and Julian got back together."

"That's a cop out. I was a phone call away."

"I know, but you were Autumn Troy, the biggest and best publicist in the world. You had your own shit to deal with, on top of being a single mom. You didn't need to carry my burden too."

"I call bullshit."

"What?"

"You heard me. I think you didn't want to tell me because you still have a hard time letting people in your life, Kinley."

I didn't know what to say, so I kept my mouth shut.

"After all the shit that happened with your mom, I can understand, but having to go through infertil—"

"Autumn, I appreciate what you're trying to do, but there's more to it than that."

"Because of what happened that night?"

Her question didn't surprise me. She was there, his whole family was. However, I still managed to flinch.

"Listen." She stood, grabbing my hands. "All I'm saying is that I'm always here for you."

"I know."

"Christian loves you, Kinley. He'll take you any way he can."

"That's just it. I don't want him to settle for me. It's not fair to him."

"I don't want to say this, but it needs to be said."

"What?"

With an utmost sincere expression on her face, she asked, "Are you sure it's not about being scared that he's going to eventually leave you, like your mom did?"

At this point, I didn't know anymore.

We spent the rest of the afternoon talking about just how much I didn't know anymore.

18

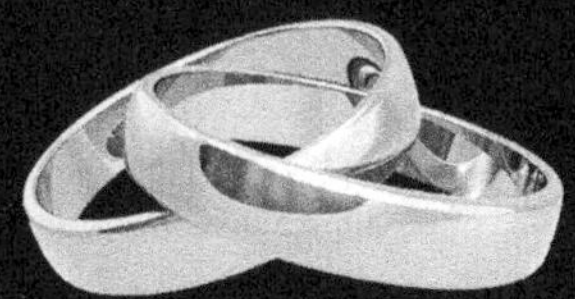

CHRISTIAN

"What the fuck are you doing here?"

I turned to see Julian standing behind me. "Exactly what it looks like." I turned back around, nodding to the bartender to bring me another drink.

"You go before the judge this afternoon."

"No shit."

"So what? You think this is what you should be doing with your time right now?"

"If you came here to bust my balls—"

He sat beside me. "Are you going to let her go without a fight?"

"I'm the only one who has been fighting for us these last few years. She doesn't want me."

"Since when has that stopped you from doing anything?"

"She's probably with Jax."

"Actually, she's with your sister."

"She is?"

Taking off his suit jacket, he nodded to the bartender. "I'll take what he's having."

"What are you doing here, man? Shouldn't you be at work?"

"I own the company. I'm where I need to be."

"Right… Alpha CEO."

He chuckled. "Don't remind me. Although, your sister has managed to change my image."

"I just saw a *Times* article calling you a coldhearted bastard."

He smiled. "I do what I can."

"How does it feel to be one of the richest men in the world?"

"Not as great as it feels to be your sister's husband and your niece's father."

"And soon-to-be nephew's father."

"Yeah," he scoffed out, taking a drink. "And that."

"What's with the tone?"

"Picked up on that, huh?"

"It'd be hard not to. What's going on?"

"I'm not going to lie to you and waste our time. I'm fucking scared shitless about having a boy."

"I'd be more terrified about having a little girl and ending up in fucking jail for all the little shits trying to get down her pants. You remember what we were like, right?"

"Exactly my point. Karma. I was a selfish bastard. The shit I put your sister through … fuck, man. Let's just say, the apple doesn't fall far from the tree."

"What's that supposed to mean? You're nothing like your parents."

"You don't know that. I don't even know that. All I'm saying is I have to raise a man, and I don't want to fuck it up."

"You're amazing with Capri."

He took another swig of his whiskey, then leaned back into his chair, and rested his glass on the bar. "I worry I won't be good enough."

I jerked back, not expecting him to say that.

"You know how I grew up, Christian. Fucking kicked around from foster home to foster home."

"Julian, look how far you've come. You're one of the richest men in the world. You have to give yourself more credit than that, man."

"I know." He nodded. "It's hard to do that, though. When I left Texas, I promised myself I'd never be that foster kid again. I threw myself into my career and didn't stop until everyone knew my name. I thought it'd give me peace."

"It didn't?"

"I don't think I'll ever have peace. In reality, I know I've made something of myself, but in my mind, I'm still that kid trying to understand why my parents didn't want me."

I bowed my head, suddenly thinking about Kinley.

We didn't talk about her mother anymore. It was one of those things we no longer discussed, it was an unspoken agreement between us. After I asked Kinley to marry me, she was left in the past. Along with that night that changed the course of our lives.

"I thought it would eventually go away, but when we found out we were having a boy, it resurfaced all this PTSD bullshit I didn't know I still had."

"You're an amazing father. Boy or girl, you have nothing to worry about."

"It doesn't feel that way to me." He eyed me skeptically. "What?"

"Nothing." I shook my head.

"It's not nothing. What's up?"

"I never told you this, but my initial pull toward Kinley was the fact that she reminded me a lot of you. Now hearing you say all this, I can't help but wonder if that's how she feels. Like she'll never be good enough for me."

"There's a big difference between Kinley and me, Christian. I had strangers tell me I was worthless and that they didn't want me. With her, it was her own mother telling her those things."

His words weighed heavy on my heart. I hadn't seen her since we signed the divorce papers. We were both avoiding each other. There was nothing left to say, we'd said it all.

"That shit stays with you, Christian. For a long time, I worked my life away. And I think a huge part of you was doing the same. You had the beautiful wife, the perfect house, you're a successful doctor, you have everything you ever wanted, yet it wasn't enough. I think you need to ask yourself why it wasn't."

"I already know." I paused, needing a second to be honest with myself.

Julian knew our issues of being unable to get pregnant and why. I'd told him after I started crashing at his ranch.

"I blamed her. Fuck." I shook my head. "I still blame her."

"Then why did you ask her to marry you?"

"Because I couldn't live without her. Everything was perfect between us until we started trying to have a baby, and then everything just went to shit. It happened so fast, but at the same time, it felt like it happened in slow motion. Something shifted between us. It was small at first, but after months of negative tests, somewhere along the way, the disappointment turned into resentment. Our love became tainted with the past and her choices. My resentment for her not listening to me grew, and I tried to pretend like it wasn't there, but Kinley knows me … she could feel it."

"Resentment is a bitter motherfucker. Especially when you resent yourself. I spent over ten years kicking myself in the ass for what I did to your sister. Even now, I have no idea how she found it in her heart to forgive me, but I thank God every day she did. Autumn, Capri, my son, they're my life. I'm a better man because of them. You see, Christian, you grew up with two loving parents, but Kinley didn't. She'll always be that little girl wanting the love of her mother."

"How do you know?"

"Because I'll always be that little boy wanting the love of mine too."

I thought about what he'd said for the rest of the day as the hours flew by, and before I knew it, I was walking into the courthouse, ready to once again fight for my wife.

Except the moment I saw her sitting on the bench with her head in her hands, I stopped dead in my tracks. She looked up as if she felt me, and the second her gaze landed on mine, she started bawling her eyes out. Her beautiful face was filled with so much despair and sadness that it caused a physical reaction from me.

The ache I felt in my heart was beyond crippling.

I was at a loss.

I did the only thing I could, I ran to her.

"Baby," I coaxed, crouching in front of her on the bench. "I'm here, sweetness. I'm here."

"Christian…"

She looked down at me with a huge hollow vacancy in her eyes while I pulled her hair away from her face.

"It's not too late, Kinley. We don't have to do this. We can tear up these papers right now and walk out of here together. I know it's going to take work to fix what's happened between us. We'll fight again. You'll call me an asshole, and I'll tell you you're being a pain in my ass."

She softly chuckled.

"But I want that with you. Now, tomorrow, a month from now, a year, forever. You're my home—you'll always be my home." I kissed her hands. "I'm sorry for not making you more of a priority. I'm sorry for not listening to your needs and wants. I'm sorry for not being a better husband. I'm so fucking sorry for everything, baby."

"I know. I'm sorry too. I've been far from perfect these last couple of years, and you've been nothing but good to me since the first time we talked. I never thought I'd have a man like you in my life. You're better than anything I could have dreamed of."

The air was so thick between us that I found it hard to breathe, not knowing where this was going.

Hoping.

Praying.

"From the moment I laid my eyes on you, all I've ever wanted was to make you happy. You know that, don't you?"

"Yes."

"These last two months, I've done a lot of thinking. For the first time in my life, I felt lost without you by my side. I don't recognize the man I've become, Kinley, and I've been trying to find him. That man. The one you met. The one you loved. The one who was made for only you. I couldn't find him, but the more I searched, the harder it was to accept I may never be him again. Because he doesn't exist without you."

She leaned in to my touch.

"The truth is I do resent you, Kinley."

She grimaced, not trying to hide it.

"I didn't want to admit it to myself, let alone you. Julian found me at the bar this afternoon, and after talking to him, I realized how much I still didn't understand what you went through—what you were, are going through.

I guess I thought I'd healed you."

"You did, Christian. I don't know where I would be without you."

"We've both made mistakes, and I'm ready to stop living in the things we can't change. If we can't have kids, then it is what it is. We live another life, maybe get a puppy."

She choked out a laugh. "You don't want a baby anymore?"

"I want you. That's what I want. Now please tell me you've changed your mind and we're not going through with this. Please, baby."

What happened next could only be described as a moment where God finally heard our prayers.

She declared, "I'm pregnant."

19

CHRISTIAN

With the wind knocked out of me, I replied, "I'm sorry, what?"

She didn't hesitate in repeating, "I'm pregnant."

"With a baby?"

"Yes." She smiled. "With your baby. Our baby."

Was I hallucinating?

"Wait, how?"

"Christian, you're an OB-GYN." She smirked. "You know how babies are made."

"Kinley, don't tease me. When did this happen?"

"The night you came over. I'm not really sure which one of those times it was, considering you were inside me most of the night, but it was definitely that night."

"Are you sure? How long have you known?"

"I found out this morning when your sister came over and we just started talking. She asked how I was doing, and I told her I felt horrible. I was tired all the time, no appetite, I felt like I was coming down with maybe the flu or something since I'd been sick for the past couple of days."

"Sick?"

"Yeah, I was throwing up, but I thought it was from stress or that I was coming down with something. I didn't have a fever. Maybe it was something I ate. When I was telling her all this, she looked at me like I'd suddenly grown five heads, and then out of nowhere she poked my chest, and I yelped."

My eyes widened, dumbfounded by what she was sharing.

"She asked if I'd taken a pregnancy test, and I laughed, telling her I wasn't pregnant. Well, you know your sister, she doesn't take no for an answer. I thought she was crazy to even think I was pregnant, but I still had several tests leftover from when we were trying, so I appeased her and took it for her. The second I peed on it, there was a bright pink line. I thought I was imagining it at first, wanting to see that line for so many years now. But when I showed it to Autumn, she immediately started crying. I swear I drank like a gallon of water and peed on ten more." She opened her purse, showing me the tests. "They're all positive."

Silence.

"Christian, did you hear what I said?"

I nodded.

"Are you okay?"

I nodded again.

"You don't look like you're okay."

I held my finger up in the air. "I'm just trying to process all this."

"I know. I can't believe it either. I'm pregnant!"

I opened my mouth to reply, but nothing came out.

"This is just insane, right? Like of all the times to be pregnant, and find out about it, today of all days? It's crazy. I can barely believe it."

"Kinley, I need to check you out."

"Why? You think it's a mistak—"

"I just need to make sure everything is okay. We can stop by my office on the way home."

"Home?"

I looked around the courthouse, remembering where we were. "Fuck."

Neither one of us said anything for what felt like forever until my lawyer approached us.

"We're up next," he informed, and it was like an atomic bomb was dropped on my head.

"We're going to need a minute," I relayed.

"Yes, take your time."

As soon as he walked away, Kinley stated, "Christian—"

I cut her off. "If you tell me you still want to go through with this divorce, I will have no choice but to throw you over my shoulder and carry you out of here kicking and screaming."

I looked deep into her eyes and spoke with conviction, "Do you understand me?"

—Kinley—

I opened my mouth, but he interrupted me again. "I'm trying to remain calm, okay? Do you see how hard that is for me? But I'm doing it for you. If you for one second think I'm going to allow this bullshit of a divorce to still go through, then you're sadly mistaken. Am I making myself clear?"

"Christian—"

"Just give me a chance, okay? Just give *us* a chance. This is what we've always wanted, this has been the root of our problems, and we're finally here, on the day we're supposed to finalize our divorce. This is a sign. It's our second chance. Our fresh start. You feel it as much as I do. I know you do. I can see it in your face, hear it in your voice, feel it in my soul. You're mine, Kinley. You've always been mine, and you always will be. This"—he kissed my hand—"is our second chance vow."

I smiled. "You didn't have to say any of that. I know. It's meant to be. We're meant to be. I think this is God's way of telling us that. I don't know how it happened because the doc—"

"I don't want to talk about that, Kinley. Not right now. All I want to do is rip these papers up, throw them in the garbage, and walk out of here with my wife in my arms. That's all I need. Can you give me that?"

I didn't hesitate in replying, "Yes."

He didn't have to be told twice, he stood and called over our lawyers.

"You guys ready?" my attorney asked.

"No." Grabbing our divorce papers out of his hand, Christian ripped them up right in front of them before he announced, "We won't be needing your services anymore."

They grinned.

They fucking grinned.

"I told you," Christian's attorney said to mine.

"You knew we weren't going to go through with this?" I asked.

"Mrs. Troy," he replied. "I've been a divorce attorney for almost forty years, and I know what misery looks like. And you guys"—he looked back and forth between us—"are still very much in love with each other. I'm glad this made you open your eyes. It doesn't happen often, but it's nice to know that second chances can happen."

Christian grabbed my hand. "Thank you. Your invoices will be paid when I get back to my office."

It felt like a dream I never wanted to wake up from. We left the courthouse hand-in-hand, and I was nervous the entire drive to Christian's office, fidgeting while he said nothing. I could tell he was lost in his thoughts. However, he still reached over and grabbed my hand, knowing I needed his support.

We didn't talk. Both of us were overwhelmed by the turn of events. Our marriage was still in a rocky place, and it was going to take work to get us back to where we needed to be. But for the first time in a long time, I felt hopeful that we'd come out of this stronger, better, and more in love than ever.

The guilt I'd carried for the last ten years still weighed heavily in my heart, but there was something else now battling it.

Worry.

Could I carry to full term? Would we have a healthy baby?

As if he knew what I was questioning, Christian's hold on my hand tightened before he brought it up to his mouth to kiss it, making my heart melt. I'd been so angry at life that I stopped seeing how amazing he was to me, how much he always knew what I needed without me having to say one word.

New remorse settled over my conscience, and I tried hard to ignore it until Christian said out of nowhere, "Kinley, you know I forgive you. You're my girl."

I didn't know I needed to hear it until that very moment.

My anxiousness subsided, and once we were in the ultrasound room in his office, I felt like the walls were suddenly caving in on me.

"Christian, what if the tests were wrong? What if I'm not pregnant? Ten different tests can't be a false positive, right?"

He lovingly smiled at me, once again being my anchor like he'd been for the last twenty years. Stepping toward me, he grabbed my face and kissed my lips as his other hand moved to my panties. Hiking up my dress, he pulled my panties down a little. Never once did he stop kissing me as he walked us back to the table in the center of the room.

Gripping onto my ass, he carried me onto it, and within seconds he was down by my feet, ordering, "Spread your legs for me, baby."

I scoffed out a chuckle, knowing how much he was enjoying this. Me at his mercy.

"Let me take care of you," he added.

Even after all these years, those words still had an affect on me like they did the first time he'd said them on the Ferris wheel.

"Now be my good girl and close your eyes."

I did. My heart was beating a mile a minute.

I heard him moving around, and when I felt the probe go in between my legs, I swear I stopped breathing.

Seconds.

Minutes.

Hours could have gone by.

Until a loud, fast heartbeat filled the silence of the room. I couldn't hold back, I just reacted, bursting into tears.

Big.

Fat.

Ugly tears.

Unable to keep it in, it flew out of me like a tornado, taking down everything in its path.

I bawled for all the times we'd gotten a negative test.

For every month I told him we weren't pregnant.

For every period I got.

For every dream that was ruined after every negative test.

For the names we'd picked out and could never use.

For the nursery in our home that remained cold and empty.

For all the love we had to give, with no children to share it with.

For the home we bought with no babies to raise behind those cream-colored walls.

For all the guilt.

The I'm sorrys.

For the years that passed us by fighting.

For the little girl who was told she was worthless.

For the mother I didn't have.

For the husband I'd almost lost.

Most of all, for the baby growing inside of me…

I cried for it all.

I couldn't stop sobbing.

Shaking.

Feeling like I was dead and now revived.

My chest heaved, my lips trembled, and when I looked over at Christian for emotional support, tears were streaming down his handsome face too.

"I'm so sorry, I'm so sorry, I'm so sorry," I repeated over and over, wanting him to feel my regret, all my hurt, and shame. I threw my arms around him, wanting him to understand how truly sorry I was for what I was doing to us.

What was I thinking? How could I do this to him?

After everything he'd done for me, his love, his family, he really did heal me.

There we were.

Two broken people.

Husband and wife.

Who were trying to find their way back to one another, with a baby on the way.

Which was simply created out of pure desperation and love for each other.

20

Kinley

Then

"Happy birthday to you! Happy birthday to you! Happy birthday, dear Kinley! Happy birthday to you!"

I smiled wide, blowing out the twenty-one candles on my bright turquoise cake.

Everyone that mattered to me was there in attendance.

Christian.

His family.

Jax.

My mom.

It had been three years since she'd appeared at our graduation, and from that point forward, she was everything I'd ever wanted and needed. We had the best relationship. I saw her all the time since Christian and I attended the University of Dallas. I lived in my own apartment off-campus, near Christian and Julian's house that they rented.

Jax lived in my complex, within walking distance of my place. We were still best friends, much to Christian's disappointment. I swear he got an apartment close to me just to piss Christian off. They still butted heads over everything and anything, often bickering over the stupidest shit.

"Honey," Mom interrupted my thoughts. "You look stunning. Is that a new dress?"

"Yeah." I nodded to Christian. "It was one of my gifts."

"Christian, you have great taste."

"Thanks, Miss McKenzie."

"How many times do I have to tell you to call me Linda?"

He chuckled, winking at me.

I wish I could say his feelings toward my mom had changed, and I guess in some ways they had. He was respectful of our time together and the fact that she was in my life. However, he was still cautious when it came to her. Worrying that one day she'd hurt me again, but I wasn't.

She'd made up for all the years she wasn't there.

Always telling me how much she loved me, and how truly sorry she was for what she'd put me through. I always told her it was in the past. I didn't forget what had happened, but I'd forgiven her for what she'd done to me.

My life was pretty much perfect.

Jax wasn't as weary of my mother as Christian was. I thought she'd won him over with her cooking. She came over often to make me dinner or to help me clean up my apartment. Part of her thought I was still that little girl who needed her in that way, and I happily obliged, missing out on all the years she wasn't in my life.

I was busy with my classes. I was lucky enough to get scholarships that paid for my classes, apartment, and the things I needed, like groceries and spending money.

Next year we'd officially be graduating with our bachelors, but school didn't finish for us. I'd be going for a master's in English Literature. I wanted to be a college professor while Christian would be in his Pre-Med program for gynecology.

He wanted to be an OB-GYN, saying he couldn't wait to deliver our babies. We talked about the future a lot, getting married, buying a house, having kids. Four to be exact. Two boys, two girls. We both wanted a big family.

He was the one who spoke about children more than I did. I'd never met a man who wanted to be a father more than Christian did. I thought it was because his dad was such an honorable man. He was Christian's role model.

Christian was great with kids which didn't surprise me. He was amazing at everything.

Wrapping his arm around my waist, he tugged me toward him. We were at his parents' house, celebrating my birthday.

I always loved feeling his chest against my back. We'd spent his eighteenth birthday at a tattoo parlor where he inked our anniversary on his chest in roman numerals. It was the start of his addiction to tattoos, and he was now covered in them.

From his sleeves on both arms, down to his hands, chest, and back. It gave him this bad boy allure that I couldn't get enough of. He was a living, breathing tattooed badass who was going to be a doctor. I couldn't imagine the looks he was going to get during his internship at the hospital this summer.

He whispered in my ear from behind me, "You smell good enough to eat, Kins."

"You did get me this perfume."

"Why do you think I bought it for you?"

I spun around to face him, throwing my arms around his neck. "So you could eat me later?"

"I could eat you right now if we'd go up to my old bedroom."

"I don't think your parents would appreciate that very much."

"I've fucked you in that bedroom plenty of times."

"Yes." I kissed him. "But they weren't home, and neither was Autumn. You don't want to give your sister the wrong idea. She's fifteen now. You know she's going to start dating soon."

He kissed me back. "Over my dead body."

"Christian! Don't you want her to find love and be as happy as we are?"

"No."

"Oh my God! You're horrible."

"She's my little sister, it's my job to protect her."

"She's not so little anymore."

"She's always going to be little to me."

"Oh, come on! Don't tell me you haven't seen how much she's grown up this past year. She's gorgeous. Anytime we're together, guys' eyes land on her from across the room."

"What fucking guys?"

"Babe! Stop! She's turning into a woman, and you're going to have to accept that. Who knows, maybe she'll end up with your best friend."

His eyes widened as he jerked back. "Where'd that come from?"

I shrugged. "I don't know. I think it'd be cute. You know she has a crush on him, right?"

"She does?"

"What? She's had a crush on him ever since I can remember."

"Bullshit. She sees him as a brother."

"If you say so."

"I'm serious. Besides, Julian would never do that to me. He sees her like a little sister too. He's known her since she was born."

I smiled, repeating, "If you say so."

"Am I going to have to warn Julian to stay away from her?"

I shrugged again. "I don't think it's Julian you have to worry about." I nodded to Julian, who was sitting on the kitchen barstool, with some blonde bimbo on his lap. "He doesn't have a type, does he?"

He chuckled, "Who Julian? Are you really asking me that? You've known him for the last six years. You know he fucks anything with tits and ass."

"Oh yeah … and who do you fuck?"

He grinned, making me blush. "These tits." Roughly gripping onto my ass, he added, "And this ass."

—Christian—

Hearing Kinley talk about Julian and Autumn was fucking with my head. Later that night, I found him out by the pool, drinking a beer. His latest chick was inside, talking to Jax.

"I'd probably go check on your piece of ass before Jax steals her from you."

He looked behind me, seeing them laughing. "Let him have her. I already fucked her before the party."

"Man…" I laughed. "You ever think you're actually going to settle down?"

He shook his head. "Not made like you. One pussy for the rest of my life, that sounds like a prison sentence."

"Is that right?"

"Why are you asking me this? Since when have you taken an interest in who I have in my bed?"

"Hey, as long as it's not my little sister, I don't fucking care where you stick your dick."

He cocked an eyebrow. "Your little sister? Where did that come from?"

"Apparently, Autumn has had a crush on you for years now. You know anything about that?"

He placed his hand up in the air. "I barely talk to Autumn these days. If she's had a crush on me, I haven't noticed."

"Great, let's keep it that way."

"Christian, are you threatening me?"

"No." I smiled. "Just a warning."

"A warning for what? To stay away from Autumn?"

"You said it. I didn't."

"You didn't have to. Subtle, you're not."

"Why are you getting so defensive?"

"I'm not. You're the one who came over to me to bust my balls about your little sister."

"She's off-limits, Julian."

"I didn't know she was suddenly an option."

"She's not, and let's keep it that way."

"Duly noted."

"Christian!" Kinley hollered from the slider door. "Can you help me open this jar of salsa? It's stuck!"

"Be right there!" Looking back at Julian, I questioned, "We good?"

"Yeah. Just fucking dandy."

We clinked our beers together, and I went inside to help Kinley, keeping an eye on Autumn for the rest of the evening. The last thing I wanted to worry about was my best friend with my little sister. I had enough on my plate with constantly waiting for the other shoe to drop when it came to Kinley's mother.

Don't get me wrong, I was happy for her to have her mom in her life again, but it didn't stop that little voice in the back of my head that continuously had me worried that one day she would fuck her over yet again.

I hated that after three years I still felt this way—trying every day to tell myself she'd changed, it wasn't going to happen, that I needed to start trusting her.

My instincts about her wouldn't go away. One thing was for sure though…

When it happened, I'd be there to catch Kinley when she fell.

21

Kinley

Now

"Christian, where are we going?" I asked with a blindfold over my eyes.

"I told you. It's a surprise."

It was official, our first trimester was over, and our baby was thriving inside of my belly. I couldn't find the words to express how relieved I was that we'd got to this point and everything was still alright. I'd be lying if I said I wasn't terrified I'd miscarry. It was a miracle I was even pregnant.

I still remembered our first ultrasound after we found out we were pregnant. Christian brought me into his office after closing hours.

Once I was laying on the exam table, he ordered, "Spread your legs for me, baby."

"I hope you don't say that to all your patients, Dr. Troy?"

I didn't spread my legs fast enough, so he did it for me, winking at me. "You get the special VIP treatment, Miss Troy."

I smiled. "Good to know."

"Just try to relax for me."

I inhaled a deep breath, but going to the gynecologist was never a pleasant experience, even when it was your husband who was in between your legs.

After he was done, he stated, "Everything looks good, sweetness."

Seeing him in his doctor form was doing all sorts of things to my core, and of course he called me out on it.

"Things are getting awfully wet down here, baby."

I grabbed my face. "Christian…"

He laughed, kissing my lips. "Stop being so delicious."

The moment we heard our baby's heartbeat through the speakers, I started crying. It was such an overwhelming, beautiful sound that I never wanted to stop listening to.

I didn't know it then, but he was recording it. Later that night when I walked out of the shower, there on our bed was one of the stuffed animals he'd won me from the carnival all those years ago. I had no idea how he found it, but there was a sticker on his belly that said, "play me."

As soon as I touched it, our baby's heartbeat filled the air. For the rest of the night, he held me in his arms while we listened to our baby growing inside of me.

With my hands in his, he guided me on what felt like a boat dock.

"Stop trying to guess where we are, Kins."

I laughed, he knew me so well. "I can't help it."

He led me to walk forward, and I followed as close as I could to his warm body. I was overthinking the possibilities of what he had planned in my mind when I suddenly felt him shift. He let go of my hand, moving to stand behind me. Wrapping his arms around my shoulders, he pulled me close to his chest before removing the blindfold from my eyes.

"Open them," he whispered in my ear.

My eyes fluttered open, adjusting to the bright light. We were outside, and the fresh air and cool breeze hit all my senses.

The sun on my face.

The dock beneath my feet.

I smiled when I realized we were standing in front of a boat, named New Beginnings.

"You didn't."

He grinned. "I told you I wanted to own a yacht one day. I figured now was the right time to start making new memories as a soon-to-be family." He nodded to the front of the bow where there was a makeshift picnic like there was the night we went to the carnival all those years ago.

The view was breathtaking with the autumn colors in the sky. It looked like what would only be described as a picture-perfect postcard.

"I can't believe you did all this," I expressed in amazement, trying to hold back the tears.

"Consider this our first date, sweetness." He kissed my neck, stirring tingles to course down my spine.

I stood there dumbfounded for I didn't know how long, taking in my surroundings before stepping onto the boat with him. Christian thought about everything, down to the pack-in-play that was in the living room, and the bassinet in our bedroom.

The four-bedroom yacht was fully loaded with everything we'd need for a baby.

"I can't believe you did this," I repeated, sitting next to him. Immediately I noticed he had all my favorite foods, from desserts, to the appetizers, and even my favorite drinks. It all lined the center of our blanket for us to enjoy.

Down to the guitar he had from college. I hadn't seen it in years. He must have found it in our garage or attic. Christian picked it up as a hobby our freshman year and actually learned how to play several songs. He used to serenade me all the time. It was one of my favorite memories from our past, and I was excited he'd decided to bring it here tonight.

"I have no words, Christian Troy. You have officially outdone yourself."

"Thank you, Kinley Troy." He winked, tossing a chocolate-covered strawberry in his mouth.

"It feels amazing to be outside. God, it feels like forever since I felt the sun on my skin."

He had put a lot of thought and effort into this date, and I couldn't have been more grateful. We wanted to celebrate that we were in the safe zone of being able to finally tell his family I was pregnant. Although Autumn and Julian knew, we wanted to wait to tell his parents.

Just in case.

There were a lot of things that had changed in the last month, including Christian coming home early every evening so we could eat dinner together. We'd talk about our highs and lows of the day. It was something we picked up with Capri. She loved doing it when we'd babysit her for Julian and Autumn.

They had their hands full now—their son was born a few weeks ago.

Julian Adrian Locke II was seven pounds, six ounces, had bright blue eyes just like his daddy, and vibrant red hair just like his mommy. Autumn was in labor for an hour, no epidural. She was officially Superwoman and my hero. Their baby was the sweetest boy, and I was in love with him from the moment I saw him. The same went for Christian.

He adored his niece and nephew, and I had no worries that he wouldn't be the same with our baby.

The way his face lit up when he met their son would probably go down as one of my favorite memories.

"You look good holding that baby, Christian."

He smiled at me. "I can't wait to hold ours, sweetness."

The day continued on, and at one point I handed Christian his guitar. He asked me what I wanted him to play for me, knowing I had a few favorite songs that he used to serenade me with. It felt as though we'd gone back in time when we were just those two crazy kids who were madly in love with each other.

Christian ended up playing our wedding song that he actually performed for me during our reception. I sat there watching him with a fascinated regard, completely captivated by the man in front of my eyes. I hadn't seen him in such a long time.

The hours flew by, and before I knew it, I was leaning against his chest, watching the sunset behind the horizon while he rubbed my shoulders and played with my hair.

"I missed this."

He kissed my head. "Me too, sweetness."

I sat up, wanting to look into his eyes. "You remember what happened the last time you made me a picnic?"

He smiled. "That didn't happen at the picnic."

"We can pretend there's a Ferris wheel around here somewhere."

"Is that right?"

I winked at him.

In the past month since we had found out I was pregnant, Christian hadn't touched me once in an intimate way which was extremely unlike him. I was beginning to get a complex that maybe he wasn't sexually attracted to me right now. I was petite and was starting to show. My body was already changing, bringing on a lot of hormonal emotions I didn't anticipate this early on.

"What are you thinking about over here?"

"Nothing."

"Kinley, don't give me that. I can see the wheels spinning in your head."

Before I lost the courage, I blurted, "Why won't you touch me?"

"You sleep in my arms every night."

"I know, but I'm talking about the other stuff."

He mischievously smirked. "What other stuff?"

"Christian." I blushed. "You know what I'm talking about. You just want to hear me say it."

"And yet I'm still waiting."

I smiled, not saying a word.

"You mean why haven't I fucked you against the slider again?"

"Yeah." I smiled wider. "That."

"I want to take things slow."

"We've been together for twenty years. I'm pregnant with your baby. I think we're way past slow."

He grinned again. "Are you horny for my cock, babe?"

My eyes widened.

"Or is it my tongue fucking your pussy that you want?"

Even after all these years, Christian's ability to make me blush was still very much a thing.

"All of the above."

"I see, but I don't think that's what's bothering you."

"It's the start of what's bothering me."

"What's the rest?"

"Umm … is it me? I know my body is changing—"

"I'm going to stop you right there. It has nothing to do with your body changing, Kinley. I'd love nothing more than to fuck those tits of yours." He nodded to them. "Which are only going to get bigger as the months go on."

I didn't hesitate in asking, "Then what's the problem?"

—Christian—

I knew she would eventually bring this up. Especially since I could never keep my hands off of her to begin with. Despite knowing that having sex during pregnancy was perfectly normal and safe, it didn't stop the worry I felt in possibly hurting the baby we'd waited years for. Down to the fact that she was still high risk and I liked it rough, I was apprehensive to take her that way.

It was irrational thinking, but it was still present anytime the urge to touch her came on, and with Kinley it was all the time.

I was more attracted to her now than I'd ever been before. There was something about knowing my kid was inside of her that did all sorts of things to my cock. Not to mention, her breasts were practically spilling out of everything she wore.

"I don't want to hurt you or the baby."

She narrowed her eyes at me. "But I thought you said there was nothing wrong with me or the baby… Were you lying?"

"I don't lie to you, but you're still high risk."

"I know, but…"

"It's an irrational fear."

"Oh." She paused for a second. "How do we fix that? I'm not going to be able to go six more months without getting some."

I laughed, loving the fact she missed my dick.

"Maybe if you're a good girl, I'll eat you for dinner."

"What about you? Don't you need something for yourself?"

"Sweetness, I have you and our baby, that's all I need. But I'm not going to lie, I am thoroughly enjoying you begging for my cock."

"You're horrible!" She threw her arms around my neck for support as she straddled my waist. Nuzzling my face close to her, she rested her forehead against mine.

"I love you, Christian Troy. I'm so happy you're mine again."

I beamed, wrapping my arms around her and pulling her closer to me.

"You see, baby, that's where you got it all wrong—I've always been yours, and nothing will ever change that."

22

Kinley

Then

"Hey, sweetness," Christian greeted, wrapping his arms around my waist from behind me. I was standing outside by the pool, needing a second to myself.

I smiled, leaning into his embrace. "Hey, handsome."

"How does it feel to be a college graduate?"

"Pretty damn amazing. How about you?"

"I'd rather be in bed with my face buried in between your legs."

I giggled. "How romantic."

We were at his parents' house. They were throwing a huge celebration for all of us, including Jax and Julian who were inside hanging out. There were hundreds of people inside. The Troys were known all around Texas. His father was one of the best attorneys in the state.

"Is my mom here yet?"

"No, baby."

I could tell in his tone that he was concerned for me.

"Did she seem okay to you at the ceremony this morning?"

He shrugged, causing me to turn around to face him. "What?"

"Nothing."

"Oh, come on. I can hear it in your voice. Tell me."

"Kinley, it's our graduation. I just want to enjoy the day with you, babe."

"Are you implying what you have to say would make us fight?"

"Anything that concerns your mom makes us fight."

"That's not true. You guys have been getting along."

"Kinley, I do that for you."

"So do this for me too, and tell me what's up?"

"Fine." He deeply sighed. "But you asked for it."

"Oh my God, Christian, what?"

"I think she's drinking again."

I jerked back, not expecting him to say that. "What do you mean? Why do you think that?"

"I don't know … it's just a feeling."

"Well, your feeling is wrong. She's been sober for nine years. When are you going to give her some credit for how far she's come? You're always so hard on her."

"This" —he sternly pointed at me— "is exactly why I wanted to keep my mouth shut. Anytime I say anything about your mom you bite my head off."

"All you ever have to say is negative stuff. What do you expect from me?"

"A little understanding would be nice."

"Understanding?" I glared at him. "What would you like me to understand? That you hate my mother?"

"Kinley, I do not hate your mom."

"You could have fooled me. You know you're going to feel really bad when you realize you're wrong and she didn't relapse. And after you do, I expect a fucking apology." I turned to leave, but he grabbed my hand and stopped me.

"Babe, don't do this."

"Too late. You have no right to throw accusations around like that, Christian."

"You're right." He nodded. "I'm sorry."

"No! Now you're just saying that to save your ass. You're not being sincere with me."

think I don't realize you're out here by yourself thinking exactly what I am when it comes to her?"

"I am not!"

"Then why ask me if I thought she seemed off?"

"Because I thought maybe she was coming down with something and you saw it too! Like she was getting sick. She's been working a lot. I'm sure she's just exhausted."

"Baby…" He pulled me into his arms. "You're right. I'm sorry. I'm way off base, okay? She'll be here soon, and you can ask her yourself why she's late."

I didn't say anything. Instead, I simply hugged him back. I hated arguing with him. Today was supposed to be a day of celebration, not fighting with each other.

"Ugh! I'm sorry, Christian. I didn't mean to go off on you."

"Yes, you did, but I forgive you."

I laughed, I couldn't help it.

"Kinley!" his mom shouted from the slider. "Can you come in here for a few minutes? I want to introduce you to some family from out of state!"

"Of course!" I yelled back before looking at Christian. "You coming?"

He grinned. "I wish I was."

I smacked his chest.

"I'll meet you inside."

"You're never going to find me with all those people."

He kissed me. "I'd find you anywhere, sweetness."

"Charmer." I gave him one last kiss before making my way inside. Silently praying to God, he was wrong about my mom.

—Christian—

There were way too many people huddled together to walk in through the kitchen, so I decided to walk around the house and go in from the front door.

All of a sudden, I heard Kinley's mom holler, "Chrissstiannn!"

My gaze shifted toward the direction of her voice as she stumbled out of her driver-side door. She'd parked her car in the middle of the road in front of our home.

"Fuck," I bit to myself. Moving quickly, I made my way over to her where she practically fell into my arms.

I knew it.

I fucking knew it.

This wasn't the first time either. Her mother had been acting weird for weeks. She went from being up Kinley's ass to barely seeing her. It didn't take a genius to put two and two together. Kinley was too emotionally blind to see it. She would if she let herself though. It wasn't hard to miss.

"Miss McKenzie—"

"Hooow many timesss do I have to tells you to call meeeee Linda?" she slurred, hanging onto my shoulder.

"We need to get you an Uber home before Kinley sees you."

"Whaaat?" She jolted back, almost falling over her own two feet. "I'm heeere for my baby's—"

"You're drunk," I cut her off.

"I jussst had a little bits! You know, to celebrate!"

I shook my head, fearing the worst. Not for her…

For Kinley.

If she saw her mom like this, it would destroy her. There were hundreds of people inside, and this couldn't have been worse timing.

"You shouldn't have driven."

"Christiannnn, I'm fine."

"You're far from fine, Miss McKenzie."

"Where'sss my baby's? Where's my Kinley Care Bearsss?"

Trying to hold her upright while grabbing my phone out of the pocket of my slacks was a challenge, but I couldn't let Kinley see her mom like this. It'd break her heart, and I refused to cause her that kind of pain, today of all days. She hadn't seen her mom in this condition in years, and all I wanted to do was strangle her fucking mother in my arms for putting Kinley through this yet again.

But I was too late.

I couldn't protect her fast enough.

"Mom," Kinley coaxed, suddenly standing in front of us. Her eyes locked on the woman who was a drunken mess in my tight hold.

I'd never seen the expression on my girl's face like it was in that second, killing me slowly in the process.

"Baby's! Congratulationsssss! I'm soooooo proud of youuuu!"

"Oh my God," she rasped with wide eyes.

It was as if she was reliving her worst nightmare. Her face paled, and I could already see tears forming in her stare.

"Babe, go back inside," I pleaded, hoping she'd listen to me. "I'll take care of your mom."

Unable to resist, Kinley questioned, "Mom, when did you relapse?"

"I didnnn't relapsssse. I just had a sipssss."

My heart broke for my girl. I couldn't believe her mother could be this fucking selfish. It didn't matter how hard I tried to protect Kinley from this, it was bound to happen eventually.

"Baby, please go inside."

"Why, Mom?" Kinley questioned, her voice trembling. "Why now? You've been sober for nine years. Why did you do this to yourself? To me?"

"Everythings is alwaysss abouts you!"

"Hey!" I gripped onto her arm. "None of that!"

Her mom yanked her arm out of my grasp, immediately falling onto the road on her ass.

"Mom!" Kinley lunged for her, getting down on her knees in front of her. "Come on. Let's get you home, okay? We'll get you in a cold shower, then call your sponsor. It's fine, this is just a hiccup. You're still on your meds, right?"

"I don't knowwww. I'm tireds, Kinleysss Care Bearssss."

Fresh tears rimmed her eyes. "I know, Mom. I know."

"I'll drive your mom's car to her house, then we can take an Uber back."

"Thank you, Christian." Her tone was filled with sadness as I lifted her mom up off the ground while Kinley opened the back door to her mom's car. Carefully, I set her on the seat before shutting the door, and she was passed out within seconds.

The instant I closed my driver-side door, Kinley threw her arms around my neck and started crying.

"I'm sorry, sweetness. I'm so fucking sorry."

Tears streamed down her beautiful face, one right after the other.

"Why, Christian? Why is she doing this to me again?"

"She's an alcoholic, babe, and there's a lot of changes that are happening. I'm sure she's just trying to cope the best she can."

"I thought we were done with this. I thought this was in the past. How could I have been so stupid?"

"It's okay." I rubbed her back. "We'll get some food in her stomach, get her in a cold shower, and put her to bed. Deal with the rest in the morning."

"Okay."

I texted Julian and asked him to tell my parents what had happened, and all he could reply was, *"Fuck, man. I'm sorry."*

Kinley held my hand the entire drive to her mom's house which was about an hour away. After we finally got her into bed, Kinley didn't want to leave her, and I understood why. She was worried she'd go right back to drinking again, given the chance.

"Go back to the party, Christian. Your family is waiting for you."

I pulled her into my arms, knowing she needed me now more than ever. "You're my family, baby. I'm not going anywhere."

"Christian…"

"I know, babe. I wish I could take your pain away. The only thing I can do is be here for you in any way I can. We can try to get her into rehab or something if she agrees, but we can't make her, Kinley."

"I can't believe this is happening again. I really thought that part of our lives was over. I don't understand why she decided to ruin all the work she's put in at getting her life back together. Nine years to just fall off the wagon. Why? Please make me understand."

"I can't answer that question for you, only she can."

"I'm so sorry about earli—"

"You don't have to apologize. I'm the one who should be apologizing to you. I shouldn't have said anything. I feel horrible now that I did."

"How did you know?"

"I guess I could just tell. She went from being heavily involved in your life to barely seeing you at all. It was like she was trying to hide the truth from you."

"How did I not see it?"

"Love is blind, Kinley."

For the next hour, we cleaned up her house, finding empty bottles of vodka stashed everywhere, on top of unopened ones filling her cabinets. She'd definitely relapsed, and from the looks of it, she'd been drinking for a while. Her meds were on the counter, untouched. Standing at attention.

Kinley didn't say a word, but I could tell she was trying not to break down. Her disappointment was evident as she cried silent tears. Every couple of seconds, I heard her sniffle and breathe deeply in and out.

Once we were done getting rid of all the alcohol she hadn't opened, it was well after one in the morning. We laid down on the couch, and I pulled Kinley into the side of my body with her head on my chest. I played with her hair, trying to get her to fall asleep. I was fully aware she was mentally exhausted from the night's unexpected events.

"Christian…"

"Yeah, baby?"

"Do you think she's going to keep drinking?"

I didn't want to lie to her. All I could do was promise I'd be there for her. Although, I knew that night was the beginning of the end for her mom and her sobriety.

I just prayed she wouldn't take Kinley down with her.

23

CHRISTIAN

Now

Another month and a half had come and gone. The day we were most excited for was finally here, and we'd find out the gender of our baby. The nurses in my office knew what we were having, and they'd let Autumn know. She was adamant on throwing us a reveal party at our house.

She took care of everything: the caterer, the decorations, the invitations. There wasn't anything missing, or that she hadn't already thought of. Kinley didn't have to lift a finger. It was her day, and my sister made sure of it.

The party was better than I could have ever imagined. The theme was pirates and mermaids for our new boat and adventures. The whole house was decked to the nines. My sister had thought of every last detail that would be important in this celebration.

All our friends and family were in attendance. The house was filled with our loved ones.

The expression on my parents' faces when we told them we were pregnant was a memory I'd take to my grave. I handed them both their gifts one night when we were eating dinner at their house.

"It's not our anniversary or birthday," Mom acknowledged. "What

is this?"

"Open it and find out."

She eyed me skeptically before they both unwrapped their presents. The second my mom saw her necklace with a charm that read "grandma" and my dad saw his watch that was engraved with "grandpa," they both broke out in a fit of tears.

I'd never seen my father cry before, and it was quite a sight. He was such a strong man, so to see him fall apart was heartwarming,

"Oh, Christian, Kinley!" Mom wailed, pulling us both into a tight embrace with my dad quickly following.

We stayed there for several minutes, just enjoying this celebration for as long as we could.

Kinley looked fucking radiant, glowing from the inside out. Pregnancy truly agreed with my girl. She'd never looked better, constantly taking my breath away with her beauty and swollen belly.

Her pregnancy was good to her, and in turn she was good to me. Her hormones had made my already horny wife to incessantly crave my cock.

Mouth.

Tongue.

Fingers.

Anything with my touch, begging me to make her come. I'd never deny her the pleasure of sitting on my face, loving the taste and feel of her against my mouth. We hadn't made love again. My fear of hurting them was still alive and present in our daily life. Though my balls ached to be inside of her, I'd have to wait until the baby was born.

My touch wasn't the only thing she couldn't get enough of, eating all sorts of weird-ass cravings at all hours of the night. I didn't know where the fuck the food was going other than in her round bump. You couldn't tell she was pregnant unless she turned to the side.

I wrapped my arms around her waist from behind her, knowing how much she loved it when my tattooed chest piece was against her back. I did it now more than ever, cherishing the fact that I was holding her and our baby in my arms.

"Have I told you how beautiful you look today?"

"Once or twice, but you can totally tell me again."

I chuckled, kissing the side of her neck.

I didn't waste any more time with her. The days of coming home late were over. I was home early every night to be with her, wanting to end that chapter of our lives when she wasn't my first priority. Her and the baby were the only things that were number one in my world now, the way it should have always been.

Things were good.

We were happy.

Slowly but surely, we were letting go of the past and looking forward to the future as a family. I couldn't begin to tell you how much things had changed between us. We weren't fighting or bickering over the stupidest shit anymore. We were still seeing our therapist, trying to work out any issues that might be lingering in our marriage.

Our communication was open, honest, no longer built on resentment or guilt for the things we couldn't change. That hopeless feeling was gone, and it was replaced with a hopefulness of battling our own demons. It was easy to fall back into the love we'd always had for each other.

I focused on learning how to actually listen to what she was saying to me, making sure her needs and wants were met were my priority.

She was the love of my life, then, now, and always.

"Can we find out what we're having now?" she asked with that pouty little lip that always made my cock twitch.

"Sweetness—"

"Please… You know you want to know as badly as I do."

"I don't care what we're having, baby. I'll be happy with either."

"Well, I want a little boy."

"You do?"

"Yes. I want a mini-you with me at all times."

I laughed. "Be careful what you wish for, Kinley."

"I'm going to agree with him on that one," Jax intervened, walking up behind us and making her face light up and her mouth drop open.

"Oh my God!" She jumped into his arms. "I didn't know you were coming!"

"Of course, where else would I be? It's my girl's gender reveal party."

"She's not your girl, Jax."

"She was mine first, Christian."

"Oh, come on." She pulled away from him. "Not today, guys."

"But busting each other's balls is the way we show our affection for each other. Don't we, Christian?"

"The only affection I have for you is irritation."

He smiled. "Says the man who invited me to this party."

Kinley's eyes snapped to mine. "You did?"

I nodded. "For you."

"Awe!" She threw her arms around me again. "I know how hard that was for you. Thank you."

"I'd do anything for you. I know how much you wanted him here."

"Hey, Jax," Autumn greeted, looking from him to me. "Don't ruin this party." She stubbed her finger into my chest. "Do you understand me? I have spent the last month making sure it would be perfect."

"And it is," Kinley chimed in. "Thank you so much for putting this together, Autumn. Everything is truly perfect. I have the best sister-in-law in the whole world."

"My pleasure."

I pulled Autumn into the side of my body, kissing her head. "Thank you for everything, little sister."

"Are you ever going to stop calling me that?"

"No. You'll always be that little girl following me around. Except back then, I thought it was for me, not my best friend."

She laughed, throwing her head back.

"And thank God for that," Julian added, suddenly standing beside her.

"What's a girl to do when the guy she's madly in love with paid attention to every other girl but her."

"You weren't saying that last night when I was paying attention to your pus—"

"No," I interrupted, holding up my hand. "This will never be okay. You do not talk about what you're doing to my little sister ever. I don't give a fuck how old she is or how many kids you have. Talking about your sex life is completely off-limits."

"Have you always been such a downer?" Jax questioned, tugging Kinley into his side.

Only to have me tear her away and pull her into mine instead.

"Anyway!" Autumn exclaimed. "It's time to find out what you guys are having. Let's go outside."

We followed Autumn out and into our backyard, under the obscene number of balloons Autumn had delivered for us to take pictures with. If

I smiled for one more photo, I was going to lose my shit.

With the help of my mom, they rounded up our guests to surround us before Autumn handed each of us a smoke bomb that would tell us if we were having a boy or girl by the colors of blue or pink.

"Okay," Autumn announced. "On the count of three. Everyone counts with me! One! Two! Three!"

We both let it go at the same time, and within seconds a huge smog of bright blue filled our backyard.

Kinley burst into tears from happiness, and I pulled her into my chest.

"Baby," I whispered in her ear. "All your dreams are coming true."

We stayed like that for I didn't know how long, wanting to enjoy this moment for as long as we could. When we pulled away from one another, the expression on Jax's face was enough to immediately have me look in the direction he was.

It was only then that I truly lost my shit. Never expecting who I was locking eyes with.

Kinley's mother.

She was suddenly standing in front of us.

The fucking nerve of that woman.

—Kinley—

"Mom," I announced, almost falling on my ass from the sight of her after all these years.

I hadn't seen or talked to her in over ten years. She looked older, wearing a dress with a cardigan, her purse on her shoulder while her hair was pinned back into a low bun.

My heart was in my throat, and I instantly felt sick to my stomach. I'd be lying if I said I didn't think about her. I did often. I didn't know how to stop worrying about her wellbeing. At the end of the day, she was still my mother.

I loved her, regardless of how volatile our relationship was.

Before I could get a word in, Christian stepped in front of me and spewed, "What the fuck are you doing here?" to her.

This time I didn't stop him from treating her like shit. She deserved that and more.

Lifting her hands up in the air in surrender, she shared, "Your aunt told me where you live, Kinley. I'm just here to see my daughter and to tell you both congratulations."

Autumn and their mom sprang into action, getting our guests to go inside to give us some privacy. Jax didn't leave, not that I expected him to.

"You're not fucking welcome here, so you can turn your ass around and walk out the same door you walked through."

"Christian…"

He jerked around, getting right in my face. "No! I am not doing this shit with you again. I don't need to remind you of what happened the last time you didn't listen to me, do I?"

My chest was rising and falling with each word that flew out of his mouth while my gaze was still cemented to the woman who'd given me life. It was like I was that little girl all over again, praying that her mom would tuck her into bed.

I never thought this day would come.

Or maybe I did…

Either way, it was here, and I had no idea how to handle it.

Christian was right about everything he was saying. I felt it in the core of my being, but I couldn't stop the emotions that were wreaking havoc as to what to do with her sudden appearance in my life again.

The sad and apologetic expression on her face was tearing at my insides, one by one. I felt it in my heart, in my bones, in the pit of my stomach. The guard I had up when it came to her was breaking with her standing in front of me.

"I'm so sorry," she breathed out, hanging on by the same thread I was. "I can't tell you how sorry I am. I have no excuses for myself. The only thing I have is my profound remorse. I never meant to hurt you, either of you. Kinley Care Bear, I love you more than anything in this world. I'm asking you to please have mercy on me and allow me to be in your and my grandson's life."

Christian didn't falter, spinning around and roaring, "Over my dead body!"

Those four words.

That one statement…

Threw my mind right back to that night when I didn't listen to him.

And I'd been living with that regret ever since.

24

Kinley

Then

I blew out the twenty-four candles on my turquoise cake before Christian kissed me.

"Happy birthday, baby."

We were at his parents' house celebrating. Everyone who mattered to me was there, except for my mom. For the last two years, she was a mess. Some days were better than others. She was drinking, off her meds, and I didn't know what I could do anymore.

Christian was over it, tired of what she was constantly putting me through. On top of worrying about her endlessly, I was over at her house a lot, making sure she was at least eating, and her house was cleaned up. I was terrified she'd throw up in her sleep and choke on her own puke. I was constantly checking in on her.

The last thing I wanted was for her to die because of the decision she'd made while intoxicated.

I desperately tried to make Christian understand, and all that would end up happening was us arguing about why I was defending her, still taking care of her, and putting up with what she was doing to me.

I couldn't help it, I didn't want to lose her again. He didn't understand. His parents were normal, healthy, and they had no vices or faults. His family was perfect.

Although, at least now my mom wasn't nasty to me like she was before, always telling me how much she appreciated me, how lucky she was to have a daughter like me, how much she loved me and wished she could be better for me. I focused on that instead of the disaster she'd caused in my life.

Every day it was a different story about why she was drinking in the first place.

I was having to pick her up at random bars at all hours of the night. Most of the time I was sleeping next to Christian, who of course, never let me go on my own to get her. We'd end up in some shady ass neighborhoods with his temper looming. He was furious with her…

With me.

Yet still, he was by my side, carrying her out of the bar and into the back of his truck. One time she threw up all over his seats, and despite getting it detailed, the heavy scent of vodka and vomit lingered in the leather for several weeks. Having to throw her into cold showers to sober her up was a thing of the norm.

Let's just say Christian's patience with her was wearing very fucking thin.

I hated fighting with him over her, but what was I supposed to do? I couldn't just leave her alone. What kind of daughter would I be if one day I got a phone call that she'd died in a car accident or something? I wouldn't be able to live with myself if something happened to her and I could have prevented it.

I was at a loss when it came to her.

The only thing I could do was try to get her to take her meds. She said they didn't work anymore. She still felt manic, and the only thing that made her feel normal was drinking. She said it took away the highs and lows she was constantly battling, when in reality it was just making it worse.

I tried to tell her she needed to inform her therapist, but she'd lost her job and didn't have insurance anymore, and I couldn't for the life of me get her to fill out the paperwork for Medicaid.

It was one thing after another.

I told her I'd pay for her therapy sessions and medicine, but she was adamant she didn't want to be a burden on me, never realizing how much of a burden she was with her binge drinking. I battled my own demons, fucking petrified I'd end up like her.

It was why I barely drank, afraid I'd get addicted. It was already in my genes, adding bipolar and depression into the mix. Christian, in his medical expertise, always eased my anxiety about it, saying I'd be fine. I just needed to make sure I was always honest with him about how I was feeling daily.

His concern for me was as never-ending as mine was with my mom. I was at my wits end, not knowing which way was up or down when it came to her. It was like a rollercoaster of emotions, and I was hanging on for dear life, praying she'd eventually come to her senses and stop drinking to get her life back on track.

I started paying her bills, taking out some student loans without Christian knowing. I didn't want her to lose her home too. She'd worked so hard for it. I knew in my heart she'd eventually stop drinking, I just didn't know when or how.

"Sweetness, please try to enjoy your birthday and stop thinking about your mother."

I deeply sighed, trying to reel in my emotions. "I can't help it, Christian. I haven't heard from her all day."

"It's not the first time, babe, and it won't be the last."

"But it's my birthday, and she promised she'd be here tonight."

"Your mom makes a lot of promises she doesn't keep, Kinley."

"Not when it comes to me."

As if on cue, her car came barreling down the road. We heard her tires squealing when one of my worst fears came true. She hit Christian's parents' mailbox, running it over until her car came to a complete stop. Her body roughly jerked forward.

We all ran out of his house, hauling ass to her.

"Mom!" I shouted in a panic.

Her body was against the wheel, hunched over.

"Shit! I think she's unconscious!"

Christian was faster than I was, opening the driver-side door to see if she was alright. Her body fell into his arms, and within moments she was waking up and fighting him.

"Mom! Stop it!"

"I'm fineeee." She pitifully tried to shove him.

I grabbed her arm, holding her back. She was making an absolute fool of herself, and all I could do was stand there and let it happen. I was beyond embarrassed. This was the first time his parents, sister, and Julian were seeing her like this.

It was usually just Christian and me, and sometimes Jax. My best friend would help me take care of her while Christian was making his rounds at the hospital for his internship. He was working crazy hours, and I always felt bad that I was dragging them both into my mother's mess.

They didn't deserve it.

"Mom, you are not fine. How could you drive in this condition? What were you thinking? You could have killed someone!"

I didn't want to lose my temper, but I was furious. She was putting her life and innocent people's at risk. It was so fucking selfish. It was pointless to argue with her. She was wasted and wouldn't remember this in the morning, but I couldn't help myself.

I was exhausted from fighting a battle I couldn't win, then or now.

Christian didn't miss a beat, tearing me away from her. She couldn't even stand on her own, falling to the ground on her ass. I went for her again, but Christian held me firmly in place. He wasn't letting me go, despite me trying to make him.

"Stop it! I need to help her! Let go of me!"

He yanked me against his chest. "Stop fucking fighting me, Kinley! This ends now! You're cutting her off! Do you understand me?"

"Christian, please…" I urgently begged, knowing deep down he was right.

But I was all she had. I didn't want to lose this fight. I wanted my mother in my life.

Julian was standing behind him with Jax by his side, waiting for I don't know what. His parents were standing on their lawn, the pity for me radiating off of them, and I could feel it digging into my skin.

Shame hit my body instantly.

"No!" Christian shouted. "I am over this fucking bullshit! She could have killed someone tonight, Kinley!"

"I know! Okay?! But what am I supposed to do? She's my mom!"

"She needs consequences. She's never going to change if you're always there making excuses for her about why she's drinking to begin with. Enough is enough. She's drowning, and I can't watch you be her life vest anymore. I worry about you constantly. When I'm in class, at the hospital, it never ends!"

"I know. I'm sorry."

"I don't need to hear your apologies. What I need is for you to let her go, so she can figure it out on her own. You're not her mother, Kinley. You're her daughter. She needs to learn her role and stop thinking you're the one who's supposed to be taking care of her. You've done it for the last twenty-four years of your life. How many more years are you going to waste on her?"

"That's not fair! She's sick! How can I make you understand that?"

"I know she's sick, but she doesn't do anything to make herself better but fucking drink herself into oblivion. The more she substitutes alcohol for medication, the harder it's going to be to get her brain to work correctly again. She's self-medicating and killing herself, and the worst part is she's taking you with her and you don't see it."

"You think it's so easy to just let her go? To just cut her off? She's my mom, and I love her! She's all I have."

"Bullshit! You have me! You have my family! You have your pain in the ass best friend! You're not alone anymore. We're all here for you. We're always going to be here for you. All you're doing is driving a wedge between us by enabling your mother."

I shook my head. "You just don't get it! You have no idea what I'm going through. You have no idea what it feels like to know she's a good person. She's a great mom when she's sober and on her meds. You saw her, Christian. She's still there, that woman is still inside of her. She's just buried deep within her illness and addiction. If she won't fight for herself, then I'm going to do it for her! It's what any daughter would do!"

"Ugggg…" Mom groaned, rolling around on the ground, completely oblivious to what was happening and the war she was starting with me and Christian.

"Kinley," Jax coaxed. "Christian is right. You can't keep babying her. You're going to have to let her figure it out on her own. I know she's your mom, but what the fuck? Look at her!" He pointed to her. "She doesn't even care what she's doing to you! She barely knows where she's at right now. When is that going to compute with you?"

"Mom." I grabbed her arm, trying to get her to stand. "Come on, please get up. I'll drive you home."

"Over my dead body!"

"Christian! Stop! I'm taking her home. We can talk about this later."

"No, we're going to finish this now."

"Christian," Julian stressed, gripping onto his arm to hold him back. "Just let her be, man. It's her mother."

I'd never been more grateful for Julian than I was at that moment. Christian didn't pay him any mind, shoving him away. I hated I was now causing problems with him and his best friend.

As soon as I took a step toward her car with her in my arms, Christian snapped…

"Kinley, you're going to have to choose. It's either me or your mother."

25

Kinley

I stumbled back, his words almost knocking me on my ass. "You don't mean that."

"You get in that car with her then you're making your fucking choice. I won't stand around and watch you drown with her anymore."

All eyes were on me. I could tell his parents wanted to intervene but didn't know how or what to say. It was a whirlwind of emotions, spiraling out of control. One minute I was in his arms, feeling safe, and now I was holding my mom up with him throwing ultimatums at me.

How did this happen? What was going on? How do I fix it?

"Please don't do this…" I pleaded, feeling his anger burning a hole into my heart.

"You leave me no choice," was all Christian replied.

I didn't recognize the cold, hard man standing in front of me. He wasn't the man I'd been with for the last nine years, the one who'd protected me, loved me unconditionally, the man who'd healed me and made me believe I was worth something.

He was a stranger, standing with his fists at his side. Ready to fight for my future, not realizing I couldn't move forward with him when my mother's past was dragging me back into the Hell she'd lived in.

“Kinleyyy Care Bearrrr…” Mom slurred. “I love youuuu.”

It was all I needed to hear, the choice was made for me. I helped her into her car, buckling her into the passenger seat before getting into the driver’s side.

My heart was beating out of my chest, thinking that Christian would say something, anything to stop me, tell me he loved me and didn’t mean it. That he’d be here for me like he had been since the first time we’d talked.

He didn’t.

Not one word.

No I love you.

I’m sorry.

Nothing.

Silence.

With sorrow in his gaze, he watched as I buckled myself into the driver’s seat and never broke eye contact with me. For the first time, his stare hurt me in ways I never thought possible when it came to him. I could still feel his love, but I could also feel his hate.

I swear we just looked at each other for seconds, minutes, hours, both of us lost in our own thoughts, our own demons.

Mine was my mother.

His … was me.

He might have been my savior, but I was definitely his demise.

Slowly, I found the courage to start the car, thinking this was the moment he’d run toward me and get in to help me drive her home like he’d done so many times I lost count at this point.

Again, he didn’t.

He simply watched as I backed out of his yard, his heart breaking, his soul aching. I was taking him into Hell right there with me.

With tears streaming down my face, I looked into his eyes one last time before I drove away, leaving my heart with him…

Knowing I’d never get it back.

By the time we were on the highway, the consequences of his words started to take over, and there was a huge lump in my throat, making it hard to breathe, to swallow, to feel anything but agony for what I was putting us through at the hands of my mom.

I wanted to hate her.

Resent her.

But all I could feel was pity.

For her.

Me.

Christian.

Addiction was a cruel motherfucker. It held onto everything in its path, leaving only destruction in its wake. It wasn't comfort, it was an illusion, a cop out, an excuse to keep making bad choices. It was that voice in the back of your head, that shadow that always followed you, the devil on your shoulder, when nothing else mattered but another drink inside of you.

I knew all that, yet there I was, allowing it to control my life. You see, my mom was addicted to alcohol, and I was addicted to trying to save her life. I didn't know which one was worse. They both seemed to destroy me in the end.

I gasped in and out at rapid speed as I contemplated over and over if he'd meant it. If we were over, done, finished. I couldn't live without him. He was my everything.

"He didn't mean it," I whispered to myself, needing the false reassurance that I didn't fuck up the best thing in my life.

When all of a sudden, my mom woke up from her dead sleep. "Kinleyyyy, I can drives," she slurred, trying to grab the wheel.

"Mom, what are you doing? Stop!"

She didn't. "Go back toooo Christian'ssss, and justs let me drivee."

"Mom! Let go of the wheel! You're going to make us crash!"

I swerved left and then right, and for a moment I thought we might have lost control of the car, but when I saw that she'd fallen back into her seat, I finally exhaled a sigh of relief.

Except it was too soon.

She lunged for the wheel again and yanked it as far right as it could go.

"MOM!" I screamed bloody murder.

It vibrated throughout the entire car as my life flashed before my eyes. I slammed on the brakes, causing our car to spin in a three-sixty.

Around and around we went for what felt like hours but could have been seconds. I instinctively placed one of my arms over my face while the other landed on my mother's chest. Thinking we were going to be okay.

Choices…

We all had them.

Christian wanted me to choose him.

I didn't.

I chose her instead.

The second I realized that.

Everything. Went. Black.

—Christian—

I was leaning with my head against the seat in her hospital room, my legs spread out in front of me, and my arms crossed over my chest.

"Honey, you should go home and get some rest. You've been here for two days," Mom said.

I replied with my eyes closed, "I'm not leaving."

"Christian, you heard the doc—"

"Mom," I argued, narrowing my eyes at her.

She sighed and nodded. "I'll go get you some coffee. Do you want anything else?"

I shook my head.

Leaning over, she kissed the top of my head. "She's going to be okay."

"I know."

My body was exhausted, but my mind wouldn't stop thinking. I couldn't sleep even if I wanted to. I would remember the phone call from the hospital for the rest of my life. Years ago, I became Kinley's emergency contact. She didn't have anyone else but me.

"Mr. Troy, Kinley and her mom have been in an accident…"

This was like a nightmare I couldn't wake up from.

When I saw her, covered in bruises, eyes closed, an IV in her arm, machines blaring loudly in her room, I wanted to break down.

I wanted to switch places with her.

I wanted to make her wake up.

I felt so fucking guilty over what I'd said to her before she drove off with her drunken mother. I couldn't help but think it had something to do with the accident. I was the cause of this.

Of us.

All I had time to do was think, with a blinding headache from lack of sleep. I closed my eyes, and the next thing I knew I was slowly opening them with Kinley staring at me.

I jumped out of my chair and was over to her in two strides, grabbing her hand and kissing all over it while I hit the emergency button to let the staff know she was awake.

"I love you so much." I kissed all over her face, her mouth. "I'm so sorry, baby. I'm so fucking sorry."

Our eyes locked, both of us trying to focus and take each other in.

The RN and doctor on call made their way into the room. I stood back, allowing them more space, even though I wanted nothing more than to still be sitting by her side, holding her hand.

The doctor proceeded to check all her vitals, asking her questions at the same time. She was alert, answering each one without trouble or confusion, only easing my anxiety a little. I still felt so fucking guilty.

"My mom? Is she okay?"

He nodded. "She's fine. She's detoxing in ICU. You can see her once I get your test results back." He continued with questions until finally, they left us alone, saying he would be back with the results from her exams from earlier that day.

Once I was sitting on the edge of her bed, she expressed, "Christian, I'm so sorry. I should have listened to you."

"Shhh…" I kissed her. "I'm the one who's sorry. I should have never said that to you. I should have gone with you. You wouldn't be here if I had."

"No." She shook her head. "That's not why I'm here." I could tell she was weighing her words, and my heart was in my throat.

"I don't know what happened. She just woke up in a rage and grabbed the wheel."

My eyes widened.

The rest proceeded in slow motion. Especially when the doctor walked back into her hospital room with her test results.

Stating, "There was damage to your fallopian tubes."

I was in medical school. I didn't have to hear the rest. All I kept thinking was how I could have lost the love of my life. I came to with Kinley bawling her eyes out in my arms.

Big.

Huge.

Ugly tears.

I didn't hesitate, pulling away and looking profoundly into her eyes. All I saw was my future, with her as my wife.

I made my choice. It was her.

It was always her.

So I spoke with conviction…

"Marry me, sweetness."

26

Kinley

Now

“Mom.” I snapped out of it. “You have no idea the damage you caused that night.”

“I can only imagine.”

“No, you can’t. You want to know why? Because you ran! Like a damn coward!”

“I didn’t want to be a burden on you anymore.”

“Bullshit. You didn’t see me again because you couldn’t fucking face me, Mom. That’s what you do when the going gets tough—you run.”

“What are you talking about?” Christian asked, looking over at me.

“I never told you this, but when you left to go shower, I went to look for her. I just wanted to say goodbye. I knew she couldn’t be in my life after what had happened. I wasn’t going to lose you, Christian. I chose you.”

He jerked back, never expecting me to say that. “Why didn’t you tell me?”

“There was nothing to tell. I went to her hospital room, and she wasn’t there anymore. Even after that day, I went to your house because I just needed to have closure. To have something for everything you’d put me through, but you weren’t there either. All your stuff was gone. The landlord said you just dipped out. Your cell was disconnected. You completely dropped off the face of the earth, and I spent the last ten years still worrying about you. How stupid am I?"

"I know, but after what I did … I was so ashamed."

"Then you remember?"

She bowed her head, the shame eating her alive. "I asked the doctor how you were, and he said you were alright, and that was all I needed to know. I knew you were with Christian and his family. I knew they'd take care of you, protect you, be everything I wasn't. I couldn't destroy your life any more than I already had. I'm sorry, Kinley Care Bear. You deserved Christian and his family, not me. I left you so you could be free of me."

"Do you have any idea how hard that was for me?"

"You've always been my rock, Kinley. Even as I child, I always had you there. No matter what. And I knew that. I got sober for you. I took my medication for you. I got my life together for you. The day I realized that everything I was doing in my life was for you, I relapsed. That first drink was like being reunited with you. How sad, right? It was just a domino effect after that. I tried to take my meds, thinking they would still work, and I wouldn't be a drunk if my mind was okay." She paused, shaking her head. "I later learned that alcohol is a depressant, and for someone with my illness, it's like lighting a match to gas."

"I needed closure, Mom. It was just another thing you stole from me."

"I thought I was doing the right thing. Finally, after all these years and everything I put you through... There's so much I wish I could change in your life. So much I wish I'd done differently. I'll never forgive myself for everything I put you through."

"You have no idea what you put me through in the past ten years, especially in the past five. Your stunt that night cost me more than you'll ever know."

"I don't know where it came from. I wish I could tell you what I was thinking, but I wasn't thinking. I want you to know that I haven't drank since that night."

Never in a million years, did I ever expect for her to announce, "I went to rehab thanks to Christian."

"What?" It was my turn to jerk back from the unexpected news.

"You didn't tell her?"

He shook his head. "I didn't want to get her hopes up."

"What's going on?" I asked, impatiently waiting for their answer.

"Your husband set up a placement for me at the rehab facility that's owned by the hospital he was interning at."

"Wow," I breathed out, only looking at Christian. "You did that for her?"

He nodded. "I'd do anything for you. After I was able to set it up, I went to your mom's hospital room and told her. That was the last I heard of her. I didn't ask. I didn't want to know."

"That's why you didn't find me at my place, Kinley. I moved into the sobriety center and lived there for the next four years."

"I had no idea."

"Something changed in me that night. I didn't want to be that woman anymore, that mother. She was so broken and lost, and I finally found peace within me. I went to rehab for me, Kinley. I wanted to do it on my own, really work through my issues. I had so much childhood trauma I never dealt with. I started drinking as a teenager to cope. It was a defense mechanism. I'm still in therapy, and I have the same sponsor that I did when you were in my life. I go to AA every night, and I make sure to take my medication like clockwork. I've worked my steps for years, and now is finally the day that I want to make amends with you." She looked back and forth between Christian and me. "With both of you."

Unable to hold it in, I confessed, "That wreck you caused damaged my fallopian tubes. The doctor told us that I may never be able to conceive. We spent the past five years desperately trying for a baby. Only to wind up pregnant the day of our divorce."

"Divorce?" She narrowed her eyes at me. "Oh my God! You guys are divorced?"

"No, your daughter came to her senses." Christian rubbed my stomach. "But my boy here helped."

I smiled, despite myself.

"I'm so sorry for what I must have put you guys through. Being a parent has truly saved my life. Kinley, you're the only thing I've done right, and I will always regret the years I've wasted, but I've learned to accept them and forgive myself. I'm here today, praying that you will give me a chance and let me prove to both of you how much I've changed. I'm not that woman anymore. I don't want to be that woman ever again."

I didn't know what to say, and it was obvious that Christian didn't either. Both of us were silent, trying to figure out what the right answer was. I wanted to believe her. However, this wasn't just my life anymore. We had a son on the way, and I had to protect him.

Even if it was…

Against my own mother.

—Christian—

"Trust me, it kills me inside, and I spent years trying to kill myself at the bottom of a liquor bottle, when I should have been taking care of you. Instead of you trying to take care of me." She beamed, her whole face lighting up. "I know. You saved me, Kinley. More times than I even remember. You and Christian. I will forever be grateful to you for what you did for me. I don't think I'd be here today if it weren't for you, Christian. You truly saved my life."

I nodded, not knowing what to reply.

The only reason I set up that sober living for her was for my wife. I honestly had no idea she actually went. After I walked out of her hospital room, I never looked back. I did what I had to do, and that was the end of it. I couldn't live with myself if I hadn't done something, especially with the contacts I had at my disposal.

I never told Kinley because I didn't want my girl to get her hopes up for nothing. I was still fucking livid with her mother, and as much as I didn't want her back in our life, it was apparent she was sober, and her life was in order.

I didn't know what the right or wrong answer was when it came to her, and that was a very terrifying thing for a man like me who thrived on control. In the last year alone, life had taught me a lot of things.

"My rock bottom was almost killing us, Kinley." She pulled what looked like sobriety chips out of her purse. "I carry these with me everywhere I go, to remind myself of how far I've come."

Her eyes showed more emotion than I had seen in her even from before. Her bright green gaze intently focused on us.

"I know you're going to protect, Kinley, with everything you have, but I'm begging you to give me a chance. I'll prove myself. I know I've said this to you a hundreds, thousands, probably millions of times, but from the bottom of my heart and soul, I am so very sorry for all the damage I've caused. I needed to forgive myself from the guilt of everything I've done to you. I needed to love myself. I needed to understand why I am the way I am. It took a lot of self-discovery and therapy, but here I am, standing in front of you, pleading for another chance. I won't let you down. I'm not asking for you to forget, but I'm begging you to forgive."

My eyes shifted to Kinley, tears were falling down her cheeks. I resisted the urge to comfort her, knowing she needed to process all this on her own for a moment.

Jax and I locked eyes, I could see he was feeling what I was. Wanting to give her mother some solace. My heart was breaking for this woman, she'd been through so much and I couldn't imagine being away from my child, even if it was my fault.

I knew what it was like to not have Kinley by my side. We had our second chance, and maybe this was there's.

"I'm not saying we go back to being what we were," she added, bringing my stare back to her.

She stepped forward, grabbing Kinley's hands. Kissing them for a second. Her lips lingered on her skin as if she was trying to engrain it into her memory.

"I don't want to go back to the past. That part of our lives is done and over with. I just want to move forward in the future with you. I miss your face, your smile, your laugh, I miss hearing you say you love me."

"I know, Mom. I miss all those things too. I'm so relieved you're okay and sober. It's all I've ever wanted for you."

"I know, baby. Your love, your kindness, your heart… I'm so lucky to have you as my daughter. If we could be friends again. Start from the beginning with a clean slate. I'd love to show you my house, I own it. I'm only twenty minutes away from here. I work at the sober living facility, I'm one of their counselors. I went back to school, Kinley. I wanted to help other people go through what I did, what I still do. I can't tell you how much it's helped me knowing I'm helping others the way you did with me."

"Oh wow."

I was surprised to hear her say that.

"That's quite an accomplishment, Mom."

"Thank you, baby. I did it for myself, but I also wanted to make you proud. You're the only thing that's ever mattered to me."

Kinley took a deep breath. I wasn't startled in the least that she was hesitating. I couldn't blame her after everything her mother put her through. The emotional roller-coaster ride that was never-ending, all-consuming, held us hostage for decades.

"Can you give me another chance, Kinley Care Bear?"

Kinley's gaze connected with mine, she was waiting for what I had to say. I couldn't make this decision for her, the only thing I could mouth was, "I'll always be here for you."

She smiled with more tears cascading down her face before looking back at her mother.

With trembling lips, she cried, "We can try."

I let go of a deep breath I didn't realize I was holding. Feeling like we'd gone full circle.

There wasn't anything left to say.

To do.

I was hopeful for the future.

That included her mother in our lives.

27

CHRISTIAN

"Kinley," I warned as she kissed along the side of my neck. "We're not doing this."

"Christian…" She slowly pecked her way down my body. "Please. We've waited so long, and I'm miserable. Your son won't exit my body, and I'm overdue my delivery date! He was supposed to be here yesterday."

"You've made such a nice home for him he doesn't want to leave your womb."

I smiled, laughing. "I think that's the sweetest thing you've ever said to me."

"Kissing my ass isn't going to get you laid, sweetness."

"Ugh! Now you're just being stubborn. We haven't had sex since the night he was conceived. How are you even surviving at this point? Don't you miss me?"

"You're sitting on my stomach. What's there to miss?"

"Yes, but that's not what I'm talking about, Dr. Troy."

"Oh, so we're role playing now?"

She grinned. "I can be your dirty little secretary or your naughty nurse if you want me to be?"

"I want you to be my wife. Besides, I've had your mouth on me."

"I know, but it's not the same. Yes, I am your wife, but this is called a fantasy."

"I have everything I ever wanted. I don't need to pretend to be something we're not."

"Christian! Just fuck me!"

I laughed, I couldn't help it.

"You know that's the sure way of getting your son out of me. Please take mercy on me! I want to see my feet again, and my back is killing me. I can't do this for another day."

"But I'm going to miss seeing you pregnant."

"How can you miss it? I'm still pregnant."

"I plan on knocking you up as soon as we can make love again."

She smiled, and it lit up her eyes.

"Besides, isn't your mother coming by soon?"

"Yes, she's going to take a walk with me around the neighborhood to try to induce my labor. She's always bringing me spicy food."

In the last four months, once again, a lot had changed. After our gender reveal, and hearing her mother out, it changed something in me. Maybe it was the fact I was going to be a father now, but Kinley needed her mother, just as much as her mother needed her daughter. I couldn't continue to drive a wedge in their relationship.

Kinley needed to make her own decisions with her mom.

It started off slow at first, her stopping by, them going to lunch. We even sat in on a couple family therapy sessions with her. Little by little, my respect for her mother began growing. The effort she was putting in didn't go unnoticed.

I was ready to leave the past behind us, and solely focus on the future and our new life as a family together which included her mom in it. My girl was happy and thriving. I'd never seen her happier, and that was enough to calm my anxiety about her mother being back in our lives.

She gazed up at me through her long lashes, smirking like a fool. "You know you can never say no to me, Christian, and I'm prepared to pull out all the stops for you to give me your cock. I know your one weakness, remember?"

"The only weakness I have is worrying about you endlessly."

"Well, you don't need to worry about me anymore. You checked me out yourself."

It was true.

Last month, Kinley finally let me properly check her fallopian tubes. There was still a little damage, but nothing surgery couldn't help which was scheduled later this year. We wanted to have more kids, preferably three or four more, making up for all the years we'd missed.

I wanted her pregnant again before the end of the year.

"Baby, look at you." I rubbed her belly. "You're stuffed to the max, do you really want another big thing inside of you?"

She rolled her eyes, hiding back a smile.

"I know I'm hard to resist. It's actually more of a curse than it is a blessing. I'm just too irresistible."

She played along. "You really are."

"It's just the price I have to pay for having a huge cock."

She busted out laughing. I loved making her laugh.

"You do have the biggest dick I've ever seen."

"You've only ever seen mine."

"What kind of answer is that?"

"The only one that matters. You're up to no good."

She giggled. "But you love it when I'm a bad girl. So will my big, strong baby daddy please fill me with his huge dick? My pussy is wet for you, Christian."

"You little fucking minx. You know how much I love it when you say naughty things."

"I know. See, weakness. Now." She kissed my chest, lifting up my shirt. "As I was saying. Don't you want to take care of me?"

It was all I needed to hear, I didn't waver. Flipping her over onto her, I hovered above her.

Rasping, "Spread your legs for me, baby."

—Kinley—

He eyed me with a predatory regard I loved so much.

I smiled, cocking my head to the side, provoking him even more. "So what are you going to do with me?"

"Do you want it rough or soft?"

He grinned, arching an eyebrow. Getting closer to my face, he kissed his way from the corner of my lips, down to my chin and neck, working his way toward my breasts that were just as eager for his touch.

I inadvertently moaned. I couldn't help it. I needed him so damn bad.

"You want me to fuck you, baby?" His lips were on mine before he got the last word out, attacking every last fiber in my being. Never once letting up on his sweet torture of rocking his hard cock against my core.

"Your pouty little mouth and perfect tits. How about I fuck them first just to torture you a little longer?"

My dress was ripped off and discarded on the floor. My bra and panties quickly followed, leaving me bare underneath his touch. I tried to contain the moan threatening to escape my mouth.

He always loved me this way—naked and vulnerable at his mercy when he was still fully clothed.

Wearing his slacks, button down, and tie from work, he'd left early for me after I texted him, saying it was an emergency.

"Is this what you needed, sweetness? Is that why you called me away from work?"

My insatiable hands went to his belt, and he shot me a menacing glare as he rapidly flipped me over onto my hands and knees, much to my disapproval.

I wanted to see his face, and he knew it. He was toying with me.

"How about I fuck you from behind?"

"Up to you, but you'll be deeper that way, and your huge cock might hit our son's head."

I heard his buckle hit the wood floor as he gripped onto my hips. Tossing his shirt and slacks aside next. Using his fingers, he began rubbing my clit, and I went wild with desire.

It didn't take long until I was coming down his hand.

"There, now you're ready for me."

"Wha—"

In one thrust, he was deep inside of me, shoving my body forward and my face onto the bed.

"Fuck…" he groaned in a low, rumbling tone.

"Yes … yes … yes…" I cried out, swaying my ass, causing his cock to twitch inside of me.

He was going to have his way with me, and I was happily going to let him, over and over again.

Seconds later, he was thrusting in and out of me in a tortuous rhythm that had me coming undone. I was so wet I could hear the slapping sound of his balls against my ass cheeks with each hard thrust.

He leaned forward, brushing my hair to the side of my neck, giving him access to kiss and lick my heated, overly stimulated skin. His rigid, strong, muscular torso laid heavily on my back as I clawed at the sheets, loving the feel of his tattooed chest piece on my skin.

"Please…" I shamelessly begged, pleading with him to give me what I wanted.

"What, baby? This isn't enough? You want my fingers rubbing your greedy little clit too?"

I didn't have to answer. His hand slid in between my legs, and I couldn't hold back any longer. He was purposely trying to drive me insane.

"Oh God," I panted, my body shivering from the surprise orgasm that coursed through my veins. He continued with his assault.

Back and forth.

Up and down.

In and out his cock rammed.

"Please … please … don't stop … please…"

And he pulled out, causing me to whimper from the loss of contact. "What are you doing?"

"Relax, let me take care of you, Kinley."

Thankfully, I didn't have to suffer for very long. He placed my body where he wanted me, on the edge of the bed while he was now standing. He stroked himself to my erratic breathing as I watched through a hooded gaze.

"I missed you." I looked into his eyes, and all I saw was the love he had for me behind his bright blue-green eyes. "I missed this so much."

He slid back into me, and my head fell back against the sheets.

"Yes … yes … yes…" I repeated, climaxing all around his shaft.

Breathless.

Panting.

Moaning.

"Eyes stay on me, baby."

I gazed up at him through the slits in my eyes.

"You feel so fucking good for me this way, baby. So fucking good."

Our mouths parted in unison as he thrust in and out, making me come yet again as my core clamped down on his dick. One orgasm rolled over into the next. I couldn't stop coming.

It was only then he released a loud grunting sound, spreading his seed deep into my pussy. He stayed like that for a few seconds before he pulled out and laid beside of me.

We both lay there panting, sweating profusely.

Needing air.

Water.

Each other.

"I love you, Christian Troy."

He leaned over, kissing my mouth. "I love you more, Kinley Troy."

We stayed just like that for I didn't know how long until I stood up with his help to go clean myself off. The second I was standing, a rush of water gushed out of me.

"I know we haven't had sex in a really long time, but that can't be all your come, right?"

He laughed, pulling me into his tight embrace.

"Looks like you got what you wanted. Our son is ready to meet us."

28

CHRISTIAN

We were at my hospital in a private room, and Kinley was doing amazing. She was sucking on a piece of ice, concentrating on her breathing.

Her contractions were about a minute apart.

"Okay, baby, I need you to push for me. I can see his head crowning."

"Yes! Please! Get him out now! I'm pushing! I'm pushing!" she panted, squeezing the nurse's hand as excruciating pain ripped through her body.

"Just a few more pushes, sweetness. I need you to bear down as soon as the next wave of contractions hit. Okay?"

"I got it."

"Then hold it for a count of ten. Deep breaths in and out after. Just remember to breathe, okay? Our boy will be here before you know it."

I'd done this hundreds of times at this point, but you wouldn't think that with how nervous I was. Watching a new life come into this world was such a blessing. I'd wanted this moment for so long, and now that it was finally here, I couldn't believe it.

Kinley did what I said, grunting and groaning.

"Ugh! I don't think I can do anymore!"

"You're doing great, baby. I'm so proud of you. Only a few more pushes, and we will get to meet our son. Whenever you are ready, I need you to bear down again."

The nurse swept Kinley's soaking wet hair out of her face as she prepared to push. Things moved pretty quickly after his shoulders popped out. This overwhelming love for him took over, and I hadn't even held him yet. There were no words to describe how I was feeling. It was such a powerful emotion. Knowing we'd made this life together from the love we had for one another.

"Push, sweetness, keep pushing—he's almost out."

"Grrrr…"

"That's it, baby, just like that. He's almost completely out. Just give me one more big push."

My thoughts ran rampant, thinking about this new life coming into our lives. I was powerless to hold back the unexpected rush of emotions with seeing my son being born into the world.

Just as the thought occurred, I grabbed our son, instantly hearing, "Wah! Wah! Wah!" loud and clear in the room, instantly making his presence known.

Kinley fell back against the bed as I held our son in my arms for a brief moment before proceeding with checking him over.

"Christian, is he okay?" Kinley questioned, her voice trembling with uncertainty.

I brought him to her, laying him on her chest. "He's perfect."

Everything that happened next was in slow motion. I watched Kinley hold him close to her heart with tears in my eyes as they streamed down her beautiful face.

This day changed our lives in ways I never saw coming.

We were finally a family.

I kissed Kinley all over her face, feeling so fucking proud of my girl. "You did amazing, baby. You're such a good girl."

"I can't believe he's finally here. We've wanted this for so long."

"I know. I can't believe it either."

"I'm so sorry, Christian. For everything. I never wanted to get a divorce, I just didn't want you to not have this. I know you've wanted to be a father since we were kids."

"We're long past that. We got him, baby. We got our boy."

She smiled, kissing his head. "You have no idea how loved you are and how long we've waited for you. We love you so much, Asher."

"Asher," my RN repeated. "What a unique name, Dr. Troy. I love it."

I nodded, smiling. "It means a gift of hope."

Which was exactly what he was.

—Kinley—

Our lives had done a complete three-sixty in the matter of a week. I had everything I'd ever wanted, and it felt like a dream I never wanted to wake up from.

"Okay, Asher. Dad's here now. No more crying."

I listened to Christian, grabbing him out of his bassinet in our bedroom. It was well into the night, and he'd woke up for his feeding. Our little man had quite an appetite, practically living on my boob.

I laughed at the thought.

He cooed and kicked his chubby little legs. He listened to everything his daddy was saying, like it was the most important thing in the world. He looked exactly like Christian, making another dream of mine come true.

I couldn't help smiling at the life we'd created together. He was so fucking perfect.

"Hey, when are you going to share him?" I teased, watching as he rocked him around the room.

"We're having our man time."

"Man time, huh?"

"Yeah, I'm teaching him about all the ways of the world."

"Oh, are you going to teach him *everything* you know?"

"You mean how to make a woman beg for his coc—"

"Christian!"

He chuckled. "Your mom doesn't have to know about our man chats. It can just stay with us."

"That's not fair. I want to know too."

"You know your mom is the only woman I've ever loved?"

I beamed.

"She's had me by the balls since I was fifteen-years-old."

"Oh my God!"

"There was just something about your momma I couldn't get enough of. We've been together for twenty-one years. That's a very long time, little man. One day when you're older, I'll tell you all about how I was her first kiss, her first touch, the only man she's ever been with."

"Christian! Why don't you tell him about all the girls you've been with before me? Huh? How much you got around?"

We locked eyes.

"I don't remember anything before you, sweetness."

"Charmer."

"Let's see, what else can I tell you? Well, your mom is the love of my life. She has been since I first laid eyes on her, and you've seen your momma—she's a fucking stunner."

I shook my head, giggling.

"She's my everything. I protected her like I'll protect you. You are so loved, Asher. You're our miracle, son."

My eyes rimmed with tears.

"You're everything we ever wanted, and I can't wait to start making more memories with you. But first, let's talk about this pain in the ass named Jax."

I laughed, throwing my head back.

"I won't be upset if you don't like him."

"Wah!"

"Yeah, see, you get it. He's your mom's best friend."

I rolled my eyes. "You're my best friend, Christian."

"Is that right?"

"Mmm hmm..."

"And what does that make Jax?"

"My other best friend. I can have two, you know?"

He looked back at our son. "I think when you meet him for the first time, you should take a giant shit and throw up on him."

I laughed so hard, my stomach began hurting. "You're horrible."

"Wah!"

"I think he's hungry now. Bring him over to me so I can feed him."

"Fine. When do you think I can have your mom's tits again? Because they were mine first, little man."

I shook my head. "The things you say to him."

"What? It's our man chats."

He placed him in my arms, and for the next thirty minutes we just laid there in awe of him.

Christian was the first to break the silence. "I love you, Kinley."

I smiled, looking over at him. "I love you too."

"After all these years, I can't believe we're finally here. Do you have any idea how many times I've dreamt of this moment? Seeing you holding our baby?"

"Probably about the same number of times I did."

"This would have never happened if you didn't come over that night."

He confidently nodded. "Yes, it would have."

"Christian, we were going before the judge."

"Yeah, but I was never going to let you go. I might have signed those papers just to appease you, but I would have dragged you out of that courthouse kicking and screaming."

"Why is it that I believe you?"

"Because you know how much I mean it."

"So what you're saying is you would have kidnapped me?"

"Amongst other things."

"And what other things are you implying?"

"I would have locked you in our home until you came to your senses."

"Wow. That sounds so romantic."

"I do what I can."

"And what else?"

"You would have been my sex slave, and I would have been coming inside you, day and night, trying to knock you up until I did."

"Hmm … interesting."

"But you know what, sweetness?"

"What?"

He gazed deep into my eyes and spoke with conviction, "You wouldn't have gone through with our divorce either."

"How do you know?"

"Because, baby, you've always been mine, and there was no way you were going to forget how deep our love goes."

"I think you're right."

"I know I am."

I took a deep breath, peering at the two loves of my life. My husband and our son.

Who we made out of pure desperation when we were saying goodbye to each other.

Only to wind up pregnant…

With our new beginning.

EPILOGUE

CHRISTIAN

"You look good holding that baby," Kinley's mom stated, suddenly standing beside me.

It had been a month since Asher was born, and we were having our first family barbeque at our house. Everyone who mattered was there.

Including fucking Jax.

I kissed his head, smiling at her.

"Christian, now that we're alone for a minute, I just want to thank you again for what you did for me back then."

"My pleasure."

"I know I have said this to you so many times already, but you truly saved my life. I know without a shadow of a doubt I wouldn't be standing here if you didn't help me get into that facility."

"I love your daughter. I'd do anything for her."

"I hope one day, you can learn to love me too."

"Wah!" Asher cried out, squirming in my arms.

"I think your grandson needs a diaper change. Want to do the honors?"

"Of course." She grabbed him out of my arms. "Come here, my angel baby. Look how handsome you are."

He cooed. Our son loved her.

"You know, one day, not tomorrow or the next or even next year, but I'd love for you to eventually call me mom."

"I'd like that."

She smiled, turning around to go back inside.

Unable to hold back, I said, "Everyone makes mistakes, and I'm happy that Kinley has you back in her life. I know how much she missed you. How much she loves you."

She met my eyes. "She's the best thing I ever did."

"I have to agree."

"Thank you for loving her the way you do."

"She makes it easy."

She spun again to take a step.

"And, Miss McKenzie." I smiled at her. "I do love you. And I'm damn proud of how far you've come."

The expression on her face was enough to make a grown man cry. She didn't just light up, she fucking glowed. Almost blinding.

"I love you too." She kissed Asher's head and then made her way back inside at the same time that Kinley was walking out to me.

"What was that about?"

"Don't worry about it."

"Fine. I'll just ask my mom." She wrapped her arms around my neck. "Have I told you how much I love you today?"

"Yes, but you know how much I love to hear it."

"I love you, Christian."

"I love you more, sweetness."

"Not possible."

I gripped onto her ass, sitting her up on the outside kitchen counter to stand in between her legs.

"I can't wait to get you pregnant again."

"Oh my God! We just had a baby a month ago."

"I know, and I'm ready for the next."

"I'm not if you won't put out for nine months."

"Well, you also know how much I love you begging for my cock."

She giggled, and it was still the sweetest sound I'd ever heard. This was all I'd ever wanted.

A life with her.

—Kinley—

"Maybe next time we can have a little girl."

"A little girl, huh?"

"Yes." I grinned against his mouth. "One who looks exactly like you."

"But what about when she gets older and boys start calling the house?"

"Over my dead body."

I opened my mouth to reply, but Jax intervened. "You know how much I hate agreeing with Christian, but they're going to have to face Uncle Jax to get through to her."

Christian groaned into my neck, hearing him call himself Uncle Jax.

"Did you just get here?" I asked.

"Yeah, your mom handed me your son, and he shit and threw up on me."

My eyes widened, and Christian didn't miss a beat, locking eyes with him. Simply stating, "That's my boy."

I laughed, throwing my head back.

"Kinley, I thought you were on my side? Do you have a shirt I can change into? This one's covered in God knows what. What the hell are you feeding that kid?" He looked down at the huge puke stain in the front of his shirt. "How does something so big come out of something so small?"

Christian nodded to him. "I'll go see what I can find." He kissed me before he left me alone with Jax.

"Your mom looks good, Kinley."

"I know. Asher is obsessed with her. She's the only one who can get him to stop crying. She's like the baby whisperer."

"Motherhood suits you. You've never looked better."

"I wish I could say the same to you."

He sighed. "Am I that obvious?"

"I've known you since I was twelve. You have that look about you. Is something wrong?"

He leaned against the counter with his hands gripping the edge, and the expression on his face quickly turned into one I hadn't seen before. It instantly made me worry.

"What, Jax? You're freaking me out."

"I know. I don't know how to say it other than…" He hesitated before confessing…

"I royally fucked up, Kinley. And now I need your help."

The end.

For Christian and Kinley.

It's only the beginning or is it *the end* for …
Jax Colton.

I was the eternal bachelor.
Until the day came when life bit me in the ass. All I could say was karma was a real son of a bitch.

Second Chance Scandal (Standalone/Second Chance Romance)
Releasing February 16, 2022 and available for preorder now!

ACKNOWLEDGMENTS

Executive assistants & all around the reason I can write: Silla Webb & Heather Moss

Editor: Silla Webb

Cover Designer: Lori Jackson

Paperback, Ebook Formatter: Silla Webb

Publicist: Danielle Sanchez

Agent: Stephanie DeLamater Phillips

Bloggers/Bookstagrammers: Without you I'd be nothing. Thank you for all your support always.

My VIPS/Readers

Photographer: Algarin Studio

Cover Model: Micah P Truitt

Street Team Leaders: Leeann Van Rensburg & Jamie Guellar

Teasers & Promo: Heather Moss, Silla Webb, & Shereads.pang

My VIP Reader Group Admins:

Lily Garcia, Leeann Van Rensburg, Jennifer Pon, Jessica Laws, Louisa Brandenburger

Street Team & Hype Girls: You're the best.

My alphas & betas:

Thank you for helping me bring this book to life.

MEET M. ROBINSON

Wall Street Journal & USA Today Bestselling Author M. Robinson loves her readers more than anything! They have given her the title of the 'Queen of Angst.' With several bestselling novels under her belt, she loves to write and couldn't imagine doing anything else with her life.

Her readers are everything to her and she loves to connect with her following through all her social media platforms, also through email! Please keep in touch in her reader group VIP on Facebook, if she's not in there than she is on Instagram or her author Facebook page.

She lives in Brandon Fl with the love of her life, her lobster, and husband Bossman. They have one Wheaten Terrier, a Miniature Cockapoo, and a user Tabby cat. She is extremely close to her family, and when she isn't living the cave life writing her epic love stories, she is spending money shopping or living boat life. Anywhere and everywhere. She loves reading and spending time with her family and friends whenever she can.

She truly appreciates her readers being on this writing journey with her. She thanks God every day that this is her life of telling stories to make people feel and disappear to another world.

Being an author is her first passion in life. It was what she was meant to do on this earth. Be a portal for characters who want their stories told.

MORE BOOKS BY M

SECOND CHANCE ROMANCE

Second Chance Contract
Second Chance Vow
Second Chance Scandal

ANGSTY ROM-COM

The Kiss
The Fling

MAFIA/ORGANIZED CRIME ROMANCE

El Diablo
El Santo
El Pecador
Sinful Arrangement
Mafia Casanova: Co-written with Rachel Van Dyken
Falling for the Villain: Co-written with Rachel Van Dyken

SMALL TOWN ROMANCE

Complicate Me
Forbid Me
Undo Me
Crave Me

SINGLE DAD/NANNY ROMANCE

Choosing Us
Choosing You

ENEMIES TO LOVERS ROMANCE

Hated You Then
Love You Now

MC ROMANCE

MMA FIGHTER ROMANCE

ROCK STAR ROMANCE

BUNDLES

EROTIC ROMANCE